V. CASTRO

THE QUEEN OF THE CICADAS

LA REINA DE LAS CHICHARRAS

This is a **FLAME TREE PRESS** book

FLAME TREE PRESS
6 Melbray Mews, London, SW6 3NS, UK
flametreepress.com

US sales, distribution and warehouse:
Simon & Schuster
simonandschuster.biz

UK distribution and warehouse:
Marston Book Services Ltd
marston.co.uk

Thanks to the Flame Tree Press team, including:
Taylor Bentley, Frances Bodiam, Federica Ciaravella, Don D'Auria,
Chris Herbert, Josie Karani, Molly Rosevear, Mike Spender,
Cat Taylor, Maria Tissot, Nick Wells, Gillian Whitaker.

The cover is created by Flame Tree Studio with
thanks to Nik Keevil and Shutterstock.com.
The font families used are Avenir and Bembo.

Flame Tree Press is an imprint of Flame Tree Publishing Ltd
flametreepublishing.com

A copy of the CIP data for this book is available from the British Library
and the Library of Congress.

HB ISBN: 978-1-78758-603-1
US PB ISBN: 978-1-78758-601-7
UK PB ISBN: 978-1-78758-602-4
ebook ISBN: 978-1-78758-604-8

Printed and bound in Great Britain by Clays Ltd, Elcograf S.p.A.

V. CASTRO

THE QUEEN OF THE CICADAS

LA REINA DE LAS CHICHARRAS

FLAME TREE PRESS
London & New York

'You are the embodiment of their hate and they shall choke on it. Go forth with the brown masses of chicharras to deafen them with your mighty song. The wind blows to your favor. The wind will reduce them to faceless dust.'
Milagros Ix Chel, the Prophet – 2030

CHAPTER ONE

July 20, 2019

Past the event horizon, tears pool at my feet. They shift to form strings of dark matter that hold me together for some unknown reason. Have you ever been in a place so devoid of light you can no longer see your hands in front of your face? The darkness tricks your mind into thinking you might only be a voice with tiny thoughts like particles trying to escape a black hole. They ricochet frantically, unable to perforate the veil knitted by life events. There are no moths to eat their way through. There is no escape from that voice or thoughts that drag you deeper into a sense of not knowing what is true, or right. If this is all that is left of me, why do I still exist? Maybe I should surrender and allow myself to be sucked into oblivion. Maybe something exists on the other side.

"This is it."

The Uber driver's voice startled me from my wine haze and I snapped shut my leather journal embossed with my name on the front. It was a gift from my son for my fortieth birthday, probably chosen by his father. I use it as a place to store all the fragmented words I struggle to string together, as hard as I might try.

The imposing Victorian farmhouse was more beautiful than the photos on the website. It made me smile despite stomach cramps from drinking two mini bottles of cheap white wine on the flight, without so much as a bag of chips to absorb the alcohol. I rushed out of the car with my carry-on, down a flagstone-paved path lined with potted marigolds to the main house, which had been restored to perfection. It reminded me of a dollhouse Veronica once had. We played with blonde, blue-eyed Barbies with thighs that never touched. The dollhouse was the perfect venue for the perfect bride.

There was only enough time to change and slap on a fresh coat of eyeliner and lipstick. The spaghetti-strapped satin bridesmaid's dress was reminiscent of the nineties when we hung out at Journeys and Delia's. Veronica and I chose them together, laughing uncontrollably over how old we were and how young the dresses made us feel. Veronica bought one for herself to change into for the reception. We just needed pencil-thin eyebrows that were no longer in fashion and lip liner one shade darker than the lipstick. Real chola-like. Maybe a pair of Nike Cortez or Doc Martens, depending on whether we listened to Nirvana or Selena Quintanilla at a block party. The older folks always cranked up the Tejano for impromptu dancing.

Catering staff dressed in black and white hurried in and out of the house to the barn, where the ceremony and reception would be held. I entered the open door and was greeted immediately by a young woman holding a clipboard next to a side table with a key.

"Belinda Montoya. I'm here for the wedding," I breathlessly blurted.

She ran her pen the length of the clipboard, searching through names. "Yes, you are the last one to arrive. Your room is on this floor, number six." She grabbed the keychain with a Virgen de Guadalupe charm sat on the table. "Here is your key. You walk past the kitchen to the large hallway. I believe it is the last room on the right."

"Thank you." Fuck. Last one. I walked briskly past a grand staircase in the center of the entryway leading to the second floor. My instinct was to explore; however, I needed to change as quickly as possible. Once inside my room, I undressed, catching myself in the full-length, free-standing mirror. My C-section scar stared back like a malicious smile just above my panty line. The red rings around my nipples resembled bloodshot eyes even a year after my augmentation. What a stupid fairy tale, or more like urban legend, that tells us time heals all wounds. No, it doesn't. Scars don't ever really heal. My skin was a mere bag to hold my tears and alcohol. Without Botox, dermal fillers, and other various procedures to halt my slow decay, I was afraid of the fright my reflection would be. I had so many more advantages than my mother and the women before her, but the sadness and longing lingered. We were from different generations of brokenness, not experiencing enough love. When you don't know what that is, you will look for it everywhere. The more immediate the hit, the better.

There I was, two divorces later, laid off (I didn't mind that as I was burned out), and a teenage kid who decided to live with his father most of the time. The older Jacob became, the less we had in common. I remember wanting a boy so badly because I feared making the same mistakes that my mother made with me. Self-esteem is a delicate thing I was sure to fuck up. All my life, my sense of self-worth amounted to less than the paper used to print my county hospital birth certificate. The first years with my boy were sweet as we baked together most days and went to the movies every weekend. He wanted me to sit for hours beside him while we put together a new box of Lego; any Lego he wanted I made sure he had. I hated and loved every second of that tedious, back-breaking play. But I was never the best cheerleader at soccer games, never really interested in knowing the rules either. Being there felt like an obligation instead of joy. Temper tantrums left me flustered, wanting to leave him at the first corner and walk away without looking back. Drowning in his shrieks, I wondered if La Llorona cried because she didn't know how to give love in a meaningful way.

I could only think of awkward things to say about girls and sex. My coordination with a PS4 controller was zero. There was no longer a welcome at the movies except to drop off and pick up, but even that was taken from me as he began taking public transportation with his friends. The first time he told me he hated me, I spat, "You don't think I sometimes hate being a mother?" I was hurt, frustrated by all the sacrifices I had made over the years for it to be like this. I wanted to be a good mother. I really tried. Nothing would stop me from believing I had failed somehow.

After putting myself together, hiding all the things I hated behind a new Tom Ford lipstick called Rust, it was time to celebrate in my home state of Texas.

I had returned for Veronica's wedding, which we planned together for months via email. Veronica was the head of the legal department for Dow Chemical. That was where she met Stewart, the nice engineer she was marrying. Unlike myself, she waited to settle down instead of getting swept up in the notion that the love and family tale could pull together all your insides like a handful of fishhooks and wire. In the end it was this very act that ripped sinew from muscle with every decision I made. Something always managed to detach sooner or later. When I was in college, watching her happiness bloom year after year made me want a do- over, or at least a couple years of therapy instead of hopping on any cock that looked like fun with a tab of ecstasy on my tongue, or whatever else was offered to me at fraternity parties. There is wild and then there is out of control. Sometimes I wonder if I was possessed in those days. Those were the days I did everything and anything to get by, to survive, to eat, stay in school, pay my student loans. Anything to claw a way out from the barrio, just like my mother did everything to claw her way out.

The wedding was a beautiful affair in the middle of nowhere with only a few close friends and immediate family. Veronica's mother, Pamela, sat perched at the front, as stunning as ever, like mestiza royalty. I didn't mind sitting quietly detached because I had done this twice and knew the drill. I surveyed the crowd, overhearing bits of conversation, realizing all their couple friends were married with children or on their second marriages trying to blend families. I guess I also kept to myself because it seemed like everyone had a plan, had things figured out. I stumbled from one life event to another in the same way I stumbled in and out of beds.

I used to pray relentlessly to God, believing in a Jacob and Isaac moment from the Bible. If I raised the blade high enough, a hand would reach down and guide it, speak to me. I guess that was why I named my son Jacob. Enough happened in my life that I continued to believe, but not enough to keep me faithful. Just like my failed marriages. My brain was stuck in a windowless room without any sense of direction. I had chosen the wrong profession but didn't know what I wanted to do at eighteen, or now. I became a mother without those things I needed to adequately parent. School didn't come easy for me at any point in time. It was only by some stroke of luck I was admitted to one college. Imagine my surprise when I received a letter of acceptance to law school. The paper trembled in my hand. I read once, twice to be sure it wasn't a trick of a desperate mind. I will go to the grave before I tell anyone how many times I took the bar exam. But I was determined to be somebody, anybody except who I was. No one told me nothing can change that. Beneath your skin and bones, something else resides, your true nature. And one thing I learned way too late in life is that just because your degree is printed on white paper, it doesn't change those preconceived notions about your brown skin.

After the dinner of filet mignon, scalloped potatoes and crisp green vegetables, the staff brought out a tiered white chocolate cake with sugared bluebonnets. Then the tearful speeches, followed by too many drinks to count from the open bar. The reception had become a huge display of everything I tried to achieve and failed to do. I grabbed a bottle of red wine from the bar and left the party in the converted barn to explore the country house where the wedding party was staying. I would crash in my bed made for one. I hated sleeping alone.

You don't see the stars in the city like you do in the countryside. I stopped midway between the barn, which emitted the joyous sounds of music and laughter, and the house, with an imposing silhouette of a single spire jutting to the sky against the brightness of the moon. Only one light in the front room remained on. In the coolness of the night my skin turned to gooseflesh. As I took a step towards the house, I felt a fluttering next to my face. I swatted the unidentifiable thing, but it refused to leave. The crickets continued to chirp despite my presence. They always stopped when disturbed. In the distance a floating glow caught my eye, a swirl of lights, blinking and congregating. Fireflies. I took a swig from the bottle and continued to walk off-balance with heels in soft grass. My gaze followed the glowing insects. Two brighter objects remained stationary in their midst. My heart quickened; the cloying frosting from the wedding cake separated from the acid in my stomach. I walked faster in my heels, which were sinking into the ground with every step, until I reached the porch.

The house was empty except for the owner, Hector, in the main sitting room. His presence made me forget my tipsy fear and the chill hovering along my spine. Men either made me feel safe or frightened the shit out of me. As hard as I tried, there was no middle ground with the opposite sex.

He sat in a creased leather wingback armchair reading *The Shining*. I knew I had to approach him. He was very good-looking, with hazel-brown eyes and black hair so thick it waved at the sides. Like I said, some things inside of us never change. My feet hurt from wearing stilettos all night and both heels were caked in dirt. I slipped off my shoes and approached Hector.

"*The Shining*. Great choice."

Hector looked up from his book to give me a smile with his full lips. "Hey, I have a thing for haunted places, and people unfortunately. Why aren't you at the party? Not that I mind the company."

I wondered if that was code for I was his type. I'm the kind of woman that harbors more ghosts and demons than Halloween, hell, and Dia de Los Muertos combined. "What other haunted places do you like?" I was trying to appear more charming than mean, bitter, floozy, drunk.

He put his book down. "You mean you don't know the history of this place?"

I took a dainty gulp of wine from the bottle and shook my head. Did I mention I'm a very classy woman with a law degree? Drinking straight from the bottle is always a sign you've met a winner. Then again, sex is sex. I think I already mentioned I hate sleeping alone.

"This place has a long history," he said. "I only know about it because one of my relatives was a farm worker who kept in touch with my grandmother. They left when things got…scary. When I got sick of trading in New York, I came down here, found this place, and decided to bring it back to life. As I researched the area, I found out my grandmother's stories from the letters she received were not just stories. The events and people were real. Ever heard of La Reina de Las Chicharras? The murdered farm worker, Milagros?"

I'm not sure if it was the wine or the sensation of gravity no longer existing, but I felt sick. Was this the place I'd heard of as an adolescent? Did Veronica know this? We spoke about the location of the wedding extensively because I found it on a wedding location website. I fell in love with the Victorian style that reminded me of something you would find in Europe. It was a two-story, fourteen-room white mansion with an octagonal tower topped with a fairy-tale castle spire on the left corner. The wraparound porch was lined with rocking chairs where I imagined Veronica and I could talk late into the evening. The barn a short walk away had been converted into a hall that could be used for various events. The high ceilings with exposed beams were restored to a beautiful burnt-orange varnish that matched the floors. Veronica wanted understated beauty with an intimate feel. I sent the link to her, but not once did she mention any urban legend tied to this place when she emailed me back to say it was exactly what she imagined. Maybe she forgot the story from so many years ago. I had forgotten it until now. Hector must have been amused by my reaction because he didn't stop with his story.

"I mean, La Llorona has nothing on her. La Reina has substantiated victims. One of her first is still alive at eighty-six. She can't move, and she's in some state hospital or home, but still. Other locals have stayed away because of the story. It's an urban legend that keeps circulating. The house was a vandalized mess when I made my first visit. It was useless for farming anymore, the land is all but dead, so people were reluctant to buy it. And no one wants to build luxury housing in the middle of rotten land. Lucky for me it's actually helped business, even if nothing supernatural's ever happened on the property. We've been featured on paranormal TV shows, podcasts. Ghost hunters from around the country have stayed here. When I reached out to the realtor, I'm surprised the bank didn't just give this place to me, they were so happy to unload it after all these years."

It didn't sound as ominous now that I was an adult. "So why did you buy it?"

"I needed a project, something creative that had nothing to do with numbers or stress. I needed to be alone. I liked the idea of a low-key country retreat. Sometimes you just vibe with things. Like I said, it was awful when the realtor drove me to the property, but I felt drawn here with a vision of what it could be."

I took a deeper drink from the bottle of wine. I wanted to see her. "What do you have to do to get her attention?"

"You look into a mirror, any mirror, and say her name once, La Reina de Las Chicharras, followed by 'chicharra' three times. I have no idea what happens next. I don't have the guts to try it."

"Let's find out if this is real." When nothing interests you anymore, you're willing to try anything that might induce a sliver of amusement. Anything to feel less numb. Fit and healthy, it would seem I had a lot of time to kill, considering I didn't have the heart to end my own misery. I took out my compact mirror from my ugly, satin, powder-blue clutch to call something I didn't think existed but brought a rush to my imagination like the night of the sleepover. It was then we heard a click and the yawning creak of a door. We both stretched our necks towards the second floor.

Hector frowned. "Hello?" He looked back at me. "I thought I was alone in here."

"What's up there?"

"More guest rooms. A bathroom I usually keep locked." We rose from our seats with our eyes on the stairs. Hector tossed his book in his armchair, then took the bottle from my hand. There was something in the way he waited a beat before drinking. He wasn't telling me something. After a long gulp, he turned to walk up the stairway. I followed him in silence. The stairs released a throaty groan beneath our steps. My hand glided against the cherry wood handrail varnished a deep red. When we reached the top, the bathroom door was open a few inches. I stepped closer to enter. Hector, however, just stood looking into the dark empty space like he'd lost the ability to move.

"What's wrong? Are you really scared? I thought you said nothing supernatural ever happened here."

"Nothing has. I swear I locked that door. Maybe one of the staff helping with the wedding unlocked it?" There was genuine concern about this bathroom for a man who claimed there was nothing supernatural about the farm.

"Are you sure you want to do this? This is the bathroom that belonged to the wife of the owner of the farm when it failed. She was so frightened by all the events following the murder she committed suicide inside there."

"How did she die?"

"She drank insecticide." His hazel eyes turned a shade darker as they quivered with fear.

I could feel the hair on my entire body rise as he uttered these words, but it was not enough to stop me. I opened the door and flipped on the light switch as we entered. Part of me expected a dingy, claustrophobic room with broken mildewed tiles and a limescale-stained sink, like in the movies. Instead, it was stylishly decorated with black subway tiles covering the walls from bottom to top, a deep brass free-standing claw-foot tub and a large oval illuminated mirror over a free-standing black sink with a fancy waterfall faucet.

I felt disgusted as I looked at my own reflection. Makeup smeared, puffy eyes full of self-imposed grief and loathing. The bruises from my top-up of dermal fillers were just seeping through my thinning foundation. If I didn't know better, I'd think *I* was the monster in the room: the failure monster, the selfish monster. My memory will never allow me to forget all the times I felt overwhelmed with my crying baby as I screamed at his shut door, "What do you want from me?" Now he was the one saying those exact same words. For a moment I hoped La Reina de Las Chicharras would climb out of the mirror like the girl in *The Ring* and take my life. That way my son would forever have fond memories of me. I took the bottle of wine back from Hector for another swig. Would she hear my call?

"La Reina de Las Chicharras chicharrachicharrachicharra."

Hector had a look of terror on his face throughout my chant. He took a step back, but not before grabbing the wine. No sound, or anything unusual, disturbed the quiet in that bathroom.

"I guess it's time for me to go to bed. Is there a Mrs. Hector?"

He placed a hand on my right shoulder. "There used to be a *Mr.* Hector, but that's over now. Mr. Hector didn't want a family and I did, more than anything. So much for thinking he would come around to the idea. All my surrogacy money went to this place instead. A different kind of baby."

I felt embarrassed and relieved at the same time. There would be no awkward walk of shame in the morning, or regret. As we left the bathroom, Hector locked it behind us. I found this very strange.

"Why lock the door if you've never experienced anything here?"

He looked at me with sad wide eyes. "Because after I gutted the entire property my grandmother told me to. Everything had to be removed. Cleansed. Then this room sealed."

I've never been one to have nightmares, but the night was racked with dreams that kept me on edge from four a.m. I imagined a woman guzzling down a bottle of insecticide, then falling to the floor foaming at the mouth, twitching like a swatted insect. But it wasn't the nightmare that disrupted my sleep. Real or imagined, I could hear flapping and scraping against my window. Since I was already awake, I dragged myself to the en-suite toilet attached to my room to relieve my wine-filled bladder. On my way back to bed I stopped at the window, parting the blinds. There was nothing but the dark. In the distance, little lights, fireflies, glowed on and off in a concentrated circle. I snapped the blinds back, thinking of the death that occurred on this farm. I was wide awake now and my phone was the only readily available distraction next to me in bed. In my curiosity I did a search on this legend and the murdered woman. It was mostly pictures of the home while it was a dilapidated pile of wood and weeds, people walking around trying to experience the supernatural. There was no information about the woman, Milagros, the supposed source of the urban legend, only the words *victim*, *Mexican*, *evil*, *woman*, *curse*. I shut off my phone and tried to get some sleep. But I couldn't sleep. My gaze fixed upon a framed antique print of La Virgen. Must be why my room key had a matching La Virgen charm. In the shadows cast from the little moonlight filtering into the room, she looked like a skull-faced Catrina. Cenotes for eyes, double pits where a nose should be and hollowed cheeks. My heart quickened. I stared at the edge of my bed, too afraid to move or close my eyes. Would something rise from below like the night of Veronica's party? I willed myself to try to rest. There was nothing in the dark except my own annoying inner dialogue. A vortex of thoughts.

I remembered the party.

*　*　*

I was twelve years old at Veronica's birthday sleepover when I first heard the story of La Reina de Las Chicharras. 'Spring Love' by Stevie B and Salt-N-Pepa's 'Push It' played on a loop from her boombox while we finished securing bright-pink sponge rollers around our bangs. The small room was filled with the mist of Aqua Net hairspray, which we applied as liberally as a roller of lip gloss – Lip Smacker in peach. I always liked going to Veronica's house. Everything seemed new, without a loose button on their sofa or a square inch of untiled cement floor. And she had her own room. My space in the world was a mattress on the floor with a few low bookcases to divide it from the rest of the living room, like a puppy with a bit of newspaper. We became good friends because she lived only a few houses down from me, and her brothers hung out with my cousin and aunt who lived with us. Their favorite game was to scare us wearing skull-faced Metallica or Megadeth t-shirts and sticking out their tongues, fingers held up in the shape of horns. There were three types of boys in my neighborhood. Metalheads with sweatbands around their wrists and long hair. You also had the cholos in Dickies with hair slicked back or shaved to the scalp. Finally, the straight from Mexico in boots made from the skin of some poor animal, well-fitted jeans and belt buckle. It was a Chicano and Mexican melting pot of single-story homes that surrounded an Air Force base. As young girls, we didn't know who we were back then; we just wanted to have fun, and there was nothing more fun than being petrified by something we *knew* didn't exist.

"Who wants a movie? We have *Nightmare on Elm Street* or *Halloween*." There was a communal sucking of teeth. We had all seen those, multiple times in fact.

"Can we go to Blockbuster and pick something else? Something new?" Luz didn't look up from working on Mona's bangs as she said this. We needed to decide fast, before bickering turned to arguing, and that would only spoil the evening.

"My mom won't take us to Blockbuster. She says it takes up too much time and she's busy getting ready for tomorrow."

The sucking of teeth turned to bobbing of heads. It was true, going to the video store was an outing all by itself. We would rush straight to the horror section to look at the new covers, flip them over to read what gory tales of the weird and fantastic we could perhaps convince an adult to allow us to watch. There was nothing more exciting than creepy VHS covers. The uglier the better.

"Mijitas! Pizza time!" Pamela, Veronica's mother, saved the day. We filed to the kitchen and dining area where, instead of pop music, the fast tongue of Spanish spoken in Mexico filled the room. A feast of cheese pizza and Big Red lay on the table for us to dig into. Abuelita Carmen looked at the greasy white and red disc with suspicion as she sat at the dining table, spreading masa on tamale husks while absently watching *Sabado Gigante* on a TV at the corner of the kitchen island. "¡Oye! You girls want to hear a scary story?"

We looked at each other, relishing the idea of being too frightened to sleep that night. The table had just enough chairs for all us girls to sit, eat and listen.

"Bueno. But it's *really* scary."

Veronica rolled her eyes. "Abuelita, we're big now. We know there's no La Llorona or La Lechuza."

The old woman shook her head of white-cropped hair as she continued to tend to her tedious work making parcels filled with shredded chili-spiced pork for the real party tomorrow. "Pamela! ¡Cervesa, por favor!"

Pamela dutifully stopped her work chopping onions to crack open a can of Budweiser. We all turned to admire the height of Pamela's teased bangs and eyeliner that was perfectly drawn on the bottom lids of her eyes. The drawing of eyeliner is as delicate and difficult a task as calligraphy or creating glyphs. She looked like a brown Farrah Fawcett the way the sides of her hair feathered out. "Last one, Mamá. This is your second."

Abuelita Carmen smiled at her daughter then took a long gulp from the cold, sweaty can. Her crooked arthritic fingers the color of wet soil shook slightly as she held the can to her lips. "Mmmm. That's better." She put down the Bud and turned her attention back to the tamales. "What is the thing you all fear the most? You say La Llorona or La Lechuza isn't scary. Tell me what is?"

Veronica, always the confident one, spoke first. "I would say rats because they're dirty and spread disease. We learned that recently in school."

Luz crinkled her nose. "No! Sharks. We saw *Jaws* and I don't want to go back to Galveston before school starts. My dad says it's not real, but still...sharks exist! They have to eat something!"

In between bites of elastic mozzarella, Mona said one word: "Hunger."

My answer was simple: to be alone, watching life happen to everyone but me. Making hard choices like my mother, damned either way because women seemed destined to be damned where I came from.

Abuelita Carmen turned to me. "Belinda, you went quiet. What about you?"

I looked into her eyes. "Death."

Her smile faded as if she could read the previous thoughts in my mind, see the course my life would take.

"Yes, death is very scary, but only because we do not know what happens next and sometimes death occurs in terrible ways to people who don't deserve it. I tell you now, death is not just something that happens. It is also a being. And girls, sometimes the dead come back to take what was stolen from them. Blood justice."

There was a silence. A bloated, gaseous silence that overtook the noise from the TV. The door leading from the back room to the kitchen slammed open.

"You're all going to die! *Aargh!*"

Veronica's brother Felipe and my cousin Juan lunged towards the table. We screamed, with our rollers and limbs quaking. Abuelita Carmen grabbed her chest with one hand and shooed them with the other as if they were strays. "¡Vamos! This isn't your party. Go!" The boys ran off, though not before they stole three slices of our pizza, laughing, with beers tucked in their black denim pockets. They were allowed alcohol if they drank at home. Usually they went to a neighboring house to visit Pimé. He was a boy their age with muscular dystrophy who could do whatever he wanted because it was no secret his life expectancy was shorter than the rest of us. Since the age of ten he had been bound to a wheelchair, but he was at every party and the neighborhood kids treated him like one of their homies. In the end he lived to be twenty-five.

Veronica put her slice of pizza down. "Abuelita, I thought Jesus said to turn the other cheek. Revenge is wrong – it's not the same as justice."

The old woman took another drink of beer and sniffed. "Caca lies. It all depends on who owns the hand that repeatedly slaps you. Bueno, chiquitas, I will tell you what *I* know of death. The year was 1952. Things were a little different then. Just a little."

CHAPTER TWO

Alice, Texas, 1952

"The fields are no place for a pretty lady, but I do like how you look when you sweat. Smell real good too."

That lazy drawl belonged to one person. Milagros looked up from her crouched position between rows of cotton to see Billy standing above her. His eyes were a perfect match for the cloudless sky and his teeth a shade of shit from the chew in his mouth. Milagros couldn't refuse to acknowledge his presence; that might mean she would instantly be let go, or something worse that she didn't want to think about. Some people felt entitled to anything they laid their eyes on. She managed to mumble, "Thank you for the job, Señor." It was one of the first phrases she learned when entering the country.

He stepped close enough that the fertilizer between her fingers couldn't mask his body odor. Milagros shuffled away from him while continuing to pull out tufts of cotton, knowing he was trying to get a peek at her breasts beneath the thin blouse she wore with faded men's dungarees. Most of the other women wore dresses that clung to their forms from sweat, but Milagros stopped wearing them when she noticed Billy staring at her just a little too long. Dungarees were more comfortable anyway. They could be tucked into her men's boots, which were the wrong size and gave her blisters periodically. Small price to pay to leave the least amount of flesh on show or exposed to the chemicals that left a painful rash. There were days her skin felt like shaved ice melting beneath the Texas summer sun.

"Well, if you ever want to come work in my house, it's nice and cool. Always got beer. If you're nice to me, I can be *real* nice to you."

A series of honks in the distance broke his gaze, which felt like a slippery tongue with tiny hands for taste buds. Both Milagros and Billy looked towards the red Ford F-Series truck. It was his wife, Tanya. The glare in her eyes was more powerful than a solar flare slapping Milagros across the face. Tanya always wore a haughty, pinched expression that seemed permanently disgusted by everyone's existence. It must have been because her ponytail was always pulled back too tightly.

Milagros looked away, trying to stifle her laughter. Did Tanya really think she wanted her pinché husband? The thought made Milagros want to vomit. She would fuck the Devil before giving Billy the pleasure. The young Baptist preacher was handsome, but she had spied him sneaking off with one of the married white ladies. Not that she would want to fuck a preacher. A holy man in the traditional sense might think he was in bed with a demon once he got to know her better. Up to now, there had been only one.

Milagros's thoughts stopped when Billy's fingers brushed against her shoulder. "We can have this conversation somewhere private later." His dirty fingernails made her want to bathe in pesticide. He left her with a wink and his shit smile at just the right angle so that Tanya wouldn't see. Another extended honk made Billy pull his hand and attention away. His cracked lips scrunched to a knot. "Yeah, I'm coming, bitch," he said under his breath as he turned to make his way to the truck.

Billy swaggered around because, in his own mind, he was a big deal running things in the fields as the nephew of the owner of the farm, Ray Perkins. Ray's wife, Betty, was also small-town aristocracy going back to the days when Texas was declared a republic. It dawned on Milagros that small towns in Mexico and here in Texas had more in common than they knew.

She glanced up to make sure he was well on his way. Tanya continued to watch her, eyes not relenting in their hateful gaze, which was no longer a slap but a bullet. It was no secret Tanya wanted nothing to do with the workers. To not arouse any suspicions in Tanya, Milagros quickly returned her attention back to work. What time was it?

Milagros could breathe again now that Billy and Tanya were driving away through a cloud of dust and out of sight. This was worker domain, cultivated by the workers' bodily fluids. Tears of frustration cut through the layer of sweat and dirt that coated her face as she ripped cotton with a ferocity she hoped might tear the plant from its roots so that it would die. She cried because her hands tingled in numbness from picking since sunrise to fulfill the terms of employment. There were endless nights of muffled sobs because she missed home, especially her twin sister, Concepcion, but every dollar meant so much to her family, who were desperate to move towns. There was no returning to her town, not after the incident. From the last letter she received, it sounded like the gossip was subsiding now that she was gone. Business for her parents never picked up again. But that no good Arturo got what he deserved. He should have left her alone. If he had listened to her, she would still be in Mexico with her family.

If only her twin was here. Together they could do something about Billy. Together they were stronger. She cried because she didn't know what she might have to do to get Billy off her back without getting *on* her back. Milagros yearned for the power to curse him and his family, who ignored the needs of the workers they relied on to make a profit on the farm. And how they loved to flaunt their profit with their nice cars and Sunday picnics with more food than they could possibly eat. It was mind-boggling how a single family could claim so much land for themselves. Milagros wondered who they'd taken it from. Her family had horror stories of their own displacement.

It wasn't just the farm that brought in the money. The family registered men through the Bracero program but charged these workers extra if they wanted to illegally bring women or their families with them. Sometimes the Perkins family would pay male workers to bring in women if there was a need. This is how she entered the country and found this farm. A friend of the family convinced her of this great new life she would have. Easy money and no taxes for her. Even her father, Julio, knew men who travelled to the US for the program. He sat with her over coffee to discuss her options.

"It started legitimate, Milagros. All those American men having to fight in the Second World War left a lot of work free. Even the women called to the factories. No one to feed the nation. I remember friends talking about how desperate the Americans were for help in agriculture. Our country and people seemed to be the solution to their problem. That was almost ten years ago. If I needed to go, perhaps I would have signed up. We were doing all right then.

Milagros trusted her father. At first the offer appeared to be the answer to her prayers; however, gratitude turned to anger when the reality wasn't anything like she imagined. It only told her she didn't really matter in this world. How are you supposed to feel about a sign that says, 'No Dogs. No Negros'? No Mexicans. She felt powerless and alone in the fields even though she was far from alone with the sweating brown workforce doing the exact same thing as she. The machine that facilitated this work stripped not only the land but all of them of their identities. They had faces, names, corridos and places they called home. Adan from Aguas Calientes, who was missing a thumb from the slice of farm equipment. Ana Maria from Veracruz, with glasses that always slid down her nose until she secured them with a tight piece of leather. Pablo from Monterrey, who played the guitar, accordion and fiddle. Elena from Guadalajara with the beautiful voice, who now dated Pablo.

Because people came and went, leaving only their name and some memory, Milagros had made only one good friend here: Guadalupe from Oaxaca. Lucky for Guadalupe, she had her brother and father to lean on at the end of the day.

The plan was, once enough money was saved, Milagros could help her family move to another town or even travel to the United States so they could be together. Milagros wanted to manifest all her hopes and dreams of becoming something more than she was in Mexico and more than a worker on a farm she had no loyalty to. She would be happy with a space that was uniquely her own, even if it was only big enough for a butterfly. Anything with wings.

Milagros ate a slice of tasteless spongy white bread and equally tasteless tinned meat. Her mother's food was always so good. Belly- and soul-filling. She sat far away from the others to be left alone, but close enough to still feel part of the group. Sometimes she went to see Guadalupe at supper or during a lunch break, but the feeling of not being welcome never left. Never had she experienced this deep sense of ghost-like vulnerability before. She listened to her brethren's conversations and songs, smelled their cooking, a melancholy reminder of home and what her future could have been.

When finished with her meager meal, Milagros only had the energy to lie down. The bedroll felt thinner tonight, making it difficult to fall asleep while thinking of Billy's hands tracing her body, that mouth full of rotting teeth and nicotine-stinking breath at her neck. She shifted to her back. Never mind the ten others under the same roof. She tented a red-and-indigo-striped serape she brought from home over her nose. The familiar scents were fading fast. Perhaps those last vestiges of the soap they made by hand infused with incantations and oils that would give you protection was all in her mind and not really there. In Mexico, her family was this serape. Here, she was a loose thread.

The free housing advertised with this job could hardly pass as a home. The aroma of body odor and flatulence was a common fog at night in their cramped, shoddily constructed bunkhouse, which caused many people to sleep outside if the weather permitted. Only once had she been in the barn where they housed the horses. It was in better condition than this place.

You had to venture out anyway if you needed to relieve yourself. Milagros was recovering from her third bladder infection caused from holding her urine to avoid leaving her bed. She needed to sleep for this work. The muscles in her shoulders required stretching to unknot before another full day of hunching over crops. Her hamstrings were in a constant state of aching soreness from squatting between the narrow rows of cotton that looked like they went on forever. Her hands, which were once smooth gloves of kid skin, were now crosshatched with scabs from field labor. At her last visit to the local clinic, she was told she appeared to be mildly dehydrated and anemic. The doctor must have felt sorry for her because he slipped her vitamins and medication for free, saying, "Our housekeeper is one of you. She is so lovely. I don't know what we would do without her. You are such good people. Take care of yourself." Milagros wondered why some kindnesses hurt. She said in her mind, *I am Milagros from San Luis Potosi.*

There were those women who placed all their hopes in domestic work. Betty, the farm owner's wife, prided herself on having the best of the bunch in the whole county to choose from. Her friends would arrive with their children running around, demanding things every five minutes while the potential domestic workers did their best to appease them even if it meant allowing them to jump all over their bodies or pull their hair. The mothers watched closely as they sipped on tea and fanned themselves, quietly pointing out their choice of help, like it was a horse show. Milagros didn't want one of those jobs, even though she had to give her personal information along with the other women on the condition of employment. It was becoming clearer by the day this other world of ownership and leisure would never be offered or open to her. Your dream could only be a dream that fits within the dream of another more worthy than you.

The seemingly constant onslaught of daylight during the summer months also made sleep just a dream, because the sun didn't truly set until after nine o'clock at night. An old bandana fixed around her eyes served as a sleep mask to block out the light so that her mind would know it was time to turn off. She imagined lying in a dark room without windows, devoid of light, somewhere she could enjoy a short reprieve from the world outside. But tonight, there were fingers of sunlight creeping in from the edges of the bandana, taunting her. A burst of laughter cut through her anxious thoughts. She shifted to her left side. Besides the sunlight and the smell, there was the noise of the camp. Workers stayed up squatting around fires, or played sad songs on the guitar about heartbreak, cooked what little food they had, laughed about things she couldn't fathom. She guessed they still needed to live even if life sometimes felt like a slow walk towards death with a single coin in your hand.

There would be no easy rest tonight after her encounter with Billy.

His advances were becoming more frequent, and bold. There had to be a way to become invisible without losing her job. Or she could hit the road. For weeks there were whispers about a man, not a curandero or a priest – a field worker. This Mexicano in California wanted to change things for them. He was a man of dreams; perhaps magic he didn't fully understand, but it worked through him for a greater purpose. Combined power is strong.

A bucket full of sea water on a wound might sting, but the dark waters of the ocean swell. It has the power to drown and knock you off your feet.

Maybe it was her destiny to join this fight. Forcing change always took a touch of the will of the gods, or God. Did it matter if it was one or many? Milagros didn't believe so. An innate belief told her human eyes were only as perceptive, or open, as the brain that controls them. Our minds were small compared to the night sky when she looked up.

Tomorrow she would write to her twin and ask for her advice. Concepcion's knowledge of the old ways was astounding. It was as if their great grandmother, Josefina, originally from Chiapas, had somehow transferred her soul to her twin upon delivery. It was Concepcion who almost died at birth. Josefina had the look of a warrior when she pulled out Concepcion with her strong forearms of lean brown rope. The look in her eyes said, *You will live, even if I have to give my life.* The baby was feet first with a cord around her neck. The scene was reminiscent of the founding of Tenochtitlan, or Mexico City as we call it now. When the wandering Aztecs saw an eagle perched on a Nopal cactus with a snake in its beak, they took it as a sign from their god, Huitzilopochtli, to build a great city there. Josefina was the eagle and the cord that had the potential to harm little Concepcion the snake. When her chest rose and fell from Josefina's breath, and the silence of the room cracked wide open with her wailing, she was declared a miracle. Some of the church ladies said it was the Devil who had hold of her. That is why she wasn't breathing and had a large strawberry birthmark on her face. The Devil's touch.

Yes, Concepcion would know a way.

★   ★   ★

The sound of the cock. A death knell every morning. Had she slept at all or just tossed and turned all night? The field filled her bones with dread and sorrow, but she would have to begin early if she wanted to make her quota so she could write a letter and get to the post office before closing. Milagros ripped off the bandana and groaned before rising from her spot. Her mouth felt dry and the slime against her teeth was a gross reminder she hadn't bothered to brush the night before. Other bunkmates moaned and moved around on their rectangular bed rolls, knowing it was time for them to rise.

Milagros quickly washed with a frigid wet rag in the ladies' so-called showers, which only sputtered cold water with negligible pressure and left enough room above and below each stall for Peeping Toms. She scrubbed her teeth extra hard. Then it was time to enter the empty fields. The red truck. Her feet refused to move any further. Was Billy here to lay claim to her? She wanted to scream for help, but there was no one around. What would she say? She tried to silence the pulse riptiding throughout her body. The sound of heavy footfalls breaking gravel and twigs behind her brought her back to the reality she didn't want to face. Before she could turn, a sharp point gnawed into the base of her skull.

Milagros shifted her eyes far enough to see Tanya and her friend, the one with pink spiderlike blotches on her cheeks and nose, closing in on her, their sour breath at each ear.

"We been waiting for you to come out. Teach you a lesson. I caught you looking at my man again, spic bitch. You know I don't like that," said Tanya through gritted teeth.

"Yeah, she don't like it. We don't like you, or your kind," chimed in the one Milagros had seen giggle with Billy whenever he was around while touching his arms at every opportunity. Once, he wiggled his tongue at this woman like a scavenged piece of roadkill hanging from the beak of a buzzard, followed by slyly touching her backside. After, she whispered something in his ear.

Milagros thought she should recount this tale to shift the blame to the real culprit, but she already knew what the outcome would be. This woman would call her a liar. There was no one to hear her, to believe her or to help her. She was alone. Faceless. Given no name.

The sharp point was replaced by a four-handed shove that pummeled her to the ground violently. Dust sprayed into her eyes and mouth from the impact that scraped her knees and palms. These injuries would make work torture today. With the strength given to her by some unseen will, she turned to face the women who stood over her.

"Look at you. Like a damn cockroach. I don't want to see you looking at my man. We married. Now get to fucking work and make us some money." The women giggled at each other.

Kneecaps throbbed. Exposed flesh burned. Dots of blood where the skin peeled away seeped to the surface, little bubbles of pain and rage. It was a wonder her entire body wasn't a rash of blood bubbles of hate that if pooled together might create a monster that would rip the innards from both women, tie their bowels around their necks like jewelry. Maybe one day. There would be no tears for them. Milagros lassoed them back in. *Hold it together, mujer, because not a one will ever cry for you.*

"Here, cunt. Since you won't cry, let me wet your face." Both took turns spitting on her, a final act of humiliation before laughing with each other as they walked away.

When they were gone, Milagros sat with bloody palms flat against the earth, allowing blood and soil to mingle, like her ancestors. Her hands trembled. She couldn't tell if it was her seething anger or the ground threatening to rip at the seams, tremors signaling the start of something ready to break forth. If only that were true. In reality, it was only the start of another day of work. She pushed herself to her feet, fighting self-pity. As she began to walk away, a flutter of wind caught her hair and pebbles rolled past her feet. She could swear she heard a female voice whisper, "I taste you."

Only a few more hours beneath the sun radiating its hot smile on their backs. Instead of her hands clenching in enmity, they curled in torment. The scrapes against her palms made picking nearly impossible as the pain increased when the digits flexed to pluck a soft ball of white. Every time she bent her knees, the skin tore a little more. Every movement cut deeper and deeper. All of this from a single shove. She would get through this and she would find the strength to write to her sister even if she had to hold the pencil between her toes or teeth.

The day ended with her picking significantly less, which she was reminded of by a foreman scowling at her. But in those hours that swung from hatred to despair, she made up her mind to leave that place before it ended her, and she was sure that it would.

At five p.m. Milagros trudged on weak legs back to her thin bed to write a letter to Concepcion.

Dearest Sister,

Life is no longer worth living if I have no prospect of living freely. I want to be free from abuse, free from fear, a little freedom to be happy. Is that not why I left in the first place? The dark nature of men's hearts has no border and God seems to have no heart, or ears. I am happy I have you to write to because you were always there for me, unlike the silent God who never seems to hear our prayers. When I seek hope, he rewards me with indifference. This is clear to me now. If I stay here, I will surely die. I have made the decision to leave this place and travel to California. I hear there is a man, Cesar is his name. I want to find his farm to join the fight. He is not a healer the way we define it, but it sounds like he is healing our people by making them stronger, their voices louder. I will leave in one week. As soon as I am settled, I will let you know where I am.

Any news of Mariposa? Mama and Papa? Take care of yourself and know I love you.

Your loving sister,
Milagros

With the letter complete, Milagros tucked it in her front pocket for mailing the next day, then made her way to the camp to find supper. Having come to a decision about her future, and written it down, gave her a sense of levity. Her intention expressed in word. It would not be easy. The idea was hardly a concrete plan. Perhaps the hidden, gods or the universe would help guide her path. This thought made her want to visit Guadalupe, see a friendly face to forget the day.

Guadalupe stood with a group of older women, chatting. Her face brightened when she saw Milagros. "My friend! It has been too long since you joined us. You know you are always welcome." Milagros and Guadalupe hugged each other. Guadalupe had short hair she could tuck behind her ears to make work easier. Milagros always knew it was her by the wide-brimmed sun hat she wore, which her mother had given her as a gift before she left.

"I know. But I have made the decision to leave. I can't take it anymore. Billy...."

Guadalupe sneered. "He is a beast. Only once did he look at me too long until he noticed my brother next to me, giving him the eyes of murder. Jose doesn't leave my side because of that disgusting man. His woman is just as bad.... Enough about them. Where will you go? You are all alone."

That word, *alone*, stung. "California. There is a man I want to meet. Cesar."

Guadalupe's demeanor changed. There was an excitement in her voice. "I hope you aren't talking about romance. Please say his last name is Chavez."

Milagros's eyes blazed in the firelight of a small outdoor grill. "Yes. Do you know him?"

Guadalupe grabbed Milagros's hand, dragging her closer to where her father served food.

"Papa, Milagros wants to go to California too. Maybe she can travel with us?"

The man, who looked to be in his late forties, stirred a stew in a cast-iron pot on a small card table before ladling it into bowls. The sun left deep grooves around his mouth and eyes and the calluses on his hands were visible. The patch of skin where his gold cross lay on his chest was lighter than the rest of him. His hair was combed to the side and his shirt sleeves were rolled to the elbows. He looked fresh from the showers.

"Well, we will be leaving soon. I don't feel safe here. And there is 'La Causa'. We all have a cause, a purpose. Even those who want to take that away or extinguish the very thing that makes us special, *our* cause. You are most welcome, Milagros, to share our dinner and travel with us. Guadalupe will give you the details."

Butterflies filled all the empty spaces inside of Milagros. "Thank you. And the stew smells delicious. I cannot wait to taste it."

What I heard next frayed my young psyche to the nerve endings.

★   ★   ★

"Mamá! Stop it!" Veronica's mother said. "They are little girls! I don't want anyone's parents calling me about nightmares." We sat in silence as Veronica's grandmother scraped the bottom of the large aluminium pot for the last of the pork, the caramelized, oily, burned bits that tasted the best.

"It's okay, Mamá, we aren't scared. Are we?" Veronica scanned our faces. We didn't know what to think or say. The story terrified me as much as it excited something inside of me.

"What should we do now?" Mona asked in a loud voice, trying to shake off the tale that was above our understanding yet scared the shit out of us. Living in a predominately Mexican neighborhood, we were too young for the burden of our skin to take root yet.

"How about light as a feather, stiff as a board?" Luz suggested.

We giggled and ran to Veronica's room with a bag of Fritos, wanting to forget the story.

That night the three of us squeezed into Veronica's bed. Luz camped on a sleeping bag on the right side of the bed. I lay between two of my friends, thinking about Milagros. I stared at my feet, not wanting to see the closet or the darkest corner of the room. As sleep was finally regulating my breathing, a shadow that wasn't there before sat at the foot of the bed. A dome the shape of a head remained firmly in front of me. I rubbed my eyes, then pinched my stomach. I was awake. I became frantic, hoping this was one of Veronica's brothers, but I would have seen the door open. It was right in front of me. I looked to my left and right and saw both friends in a deep sleep. Luz had her back turned and snored softly, still on the floor. An exhalation came from the direction of the shadow. I sat up in bed, trying to wake both of my friends to no avail. They were like floppy dolls rolling back and forth with eyes shut. As the shadow drew taller, I lay back down and closed my eyes. "No," I whispered.

The hiss stopped immediately, and I knew it was gone. I made the sign of the cross on my thumping chest and prayed for sleep.

The following morning, I awoke to the smell that could drag the dead from heaven: fresh tamales. Both of my friends were still sleeping peacefully. I survived the night and today was another party. Since it was Veronica's real birthday that day, there would be a barbecue in the backyard, and everyone would be invited. This meant sprinklers on, food to feed the armies of multiple nations, the boys grabbing empty beer cans to sneak the remnants of or shake over our heads, and music loud enough to cause neighbors to complain, but they would be over, so it really didn't matter.

The entire house was quiet when I crawled out of bed to use the bathroom, except for Veronica's grandmother singing low in the kitchen to her Tejano favorite, Emilio. I needed to know more about the story after the experience in bed. I knew it had happened and it wasn't a nightmare.

"Is it true?"

She was sitting at the table with her coffee and concha. Knee-high circulation stockings covered bulging blue and purple varicose veins. It was early, so her hair was still in a hairnet. She clacked her dentures before speaking. "I'm only telling you this because you will not always be a girl and us women are told too many lies in our lifetime, and mostly nothing good comes from those lies. Yes, the story is true."

"What will happen to me if I call her?"

"I don't know. I never wanted to try. She needs to rest. Don't worry about it, mija." She gave me a warm smile and pulled out a pink concha from a white bag. We sat at the table eating to Tejano music and the aroma of tamales.

"How's your mother? You have enough? If not, I know a few people that buy food stamps." I looked down, feeling ashamed. I knew she meant well, and we weren't the only ones on government money, receiving free breakfast and lunch at school. Two solid meals during the day and a fried bologna sandwich for dinner were more than enough. My mother was a recent college graduate earning pennies while trying to raise me.

"Yeah, she's okay. We get by. Sometimes she has to bounce a check for extra groceries or clothes, but we manage."

"And your Auntie Laura? How's her son?"

More heat on my cheeks. But we weren't the only ones with family locked up either. "Good. She's been getting extra hours at Pizza Hut. Carlos is still in juvie until they decide whether to try him as an adult or not." No one would tell me what he had done to get himself locked up. I only knew I wouldn't see him for a very long time. As it turned out, I'd be a woman before he was released.

"Your daddy?" That word was the same as if she had asked me how my potato was doing. I couldn't say he was finally gone after another affair. It was me who found the love letters stuffed underneath the front seat of the car. There was a photo of another small child that made me feel like I was somehow not good enough to stick around for. There was another one – smarter, prettier, who knows. I think her name was Clarissa. At least now my mother cried over how to make life better for us rather than over a man who only loved her enough to get what he might need at that moment. I wanted to forget the stench of marijuana and alcohol in our house at all hours and his army buddies coming in and out. I didn't know where he was or who he was with.

I shrugged my shoulders. "I don't know."

She grabbed my hand and smiled at me again with a look of sadness and defiance. Growing up, that was the Latina way. A mask I grew accustomed to seeing. There were whiskers on the corners of her mouth and on her chin, like my auntie, except my auntie plucked hers every few days, leaving her skin looking raw. My auntie did the same to her eyebrows, which were perfectly shaped arches that she filled in with a black Maybelline pencil. After a day she looked just like the women on the covers of her magazine collections. Cindy Crawford was her favorite. I wondered if I would have whiskers too when I was a woman. This was our last year of childhood, for next year we were all turning thirteen. We would wear wet n wild until we were old enough for Maybelline.

"Here, take this." She reached into the pocket of her apron and handed me a twenty-dollar bill.

"I can't."

"Yes, you will, Belinda!"

I took it and placed it in my sock. When I got home, I would hide it under a sofa cushion and pretend to find it. It would make my mother's day better, thinking God was answering a prayer. I had to believe something was out there, even if it didn't look like us. I sat at the table until the rest of the girls made their way to the kitchen for breakfast, followed by unwrapping our bangs for teasing and more hairspraying.

The party was a blast. Texas summers were meant to take away all your worries. We played outside until midnight without a care in the world as we still held on to our childhood innocence before venturing into the weird place of female puberty. I hoped that year I would finally bloom breasts after being the shortest and scrawniest of my grade.

★   ★   ★

Veronica stayed in Texas while I left as soon as I turned eighteen with three hundred dollars in my purse, which I accidently lost in a taxi while in search of a place where I could forget where I came from and be someone else. You do what you must do to survive. Abuelita Carmen lived to be ninety-eight years old. To this day my greatest regret was not going to her funeral. I was too busy trying to keep hold of love that didn't last, afraid to disrupt the precarious equilibrium in what I thought was my first healthy relationship.

CHAPTER THREE

La Virgen greeted me with her passive sad look. Her dark countenance was gone with the morning light. I felt like shit. With all the energy left in my body, I pulled myself from bed, slightly hungover. The dull ache in my head was as thick as the film of red wine that coated my tongue and teeth. Who would want to wake up next to that? As exhausted as I was, I reminded myself that today was not about me. Be like an ant and stay small. Be happy. I would have to put on my makeup and smile big for my newly married friend, then post an envy-inducing photo on Instagram so everyone would know how happy I was, so I could be reminded how happy I should be. This weekend was about Veronica, despite the fact all I could focus on was my own pain. A coffee followed by a mimosa would do the trick. An upper followed by a downer, the chemical yin and yang of life.

The bridal party met at eleven a.m. for brunch. I teetered in three-inch, red-bottomed, wedged heels to the dining room in search of coffee. Hector arranged elegant plates and cutlery with eyes as darkly ringed as mine.

"Morning. Can I get some coffee?" I asked.

He smiled, trying to appear the perfect host. "Of course, let's go to the kitchen."

He had one of those fancy Italian coffee machines that required too much effort. However, he expertly navigated the nozzles and bean crushing of a barista.

"Why don't you join me?" I offered.

"Do I look that bad? I didn't sleep at all. How about you?" He handed me a perfect macchiato.

I was so tired, filter coffee with vanilla creamer would have sufficed. "I didn't sleep at all either. I look worse than I did last night. Kept thinking about the farmer's wife, then La Reina. How about you? La Reina spook you?"

He gulped a shot of espresso. "No, my grandmother. She scolded me for opening that bathroom. It was like I was a kid again in her kitchen making tortillas. She was always scolding me for not washing my hands before helping her. My dough resembled a gray mass full of grit because they were filthy. I miss that woman. She's the reason for everything. I'm just happy I could give her a really comfortable life for her final year with us. When she was diagnosed with pancreatic cancer, she said she wanted no treatment, just let her smoke weed and die happy. That's what I did."

I liked Hector. I felt disappointed to leave the following day because he seemed like the kind of person who could be a true friend. No hidden agenda. Perhaps this was one person I could reveal the secret sadness I went great lengths to hide to not be perceived as a burden. People don't like Debbie Downers, and I wanted everyone to like me. I was the one you came to when you needed cheering up, the life of the party with bright lipstick and clothes always perfect, not the sad girl. With Hector, I saw the same melancholy in his eyes, heard it in his voice. I knew now why he doted on the flower girls, nearly in tears as he took their photos. I ached for him and his desire to be a father. I asked, "What can I do to help with this brunch?"

We ate and drank into the late afternoon until the bride and groom needed to leave for the airport. After every mimosa was emptied, I tried to gain the courage to mention to Veronica the long-forgotten birthday party and the story of La Reina de Las

Chicharras. About halfway through, the conversation moved from private schools and music lessons to only the clinking of forks, knives and the cork popping from champagne. What else do you talk about with other adults with children?

"Hey, Veronica, remember that story your grandmother told us at your birthday party? Well, more like urban legend." I kept my smile pasted to my face. The table went dead silent. The six other guests darted their heads between Veronica and me.

She frowned and cocked her head. "You mean the murdered woman?"

"Yes! That's the one. Milagros. Did you know this is the farm where it occurred?"

The silence of the table was broken by gasps and wide eyes.

"What? No way. It wasn't even real." Her response was a dismissive chuckle as she placed her hand over Stewart's. He looked enthralled.

"But it did happen, and this is the farm." Hector stood in the doorway between the kitchen and the dining room with a basket of concha.

"Okay, wait," Stewart said. "Did we just get married in a haunted farmhouse? This is amazing. What a story! So, what happened?"

Veronica squirmed in her seat, giving Stewart a sour, uncomfortable expression. "It's an awful story. Completely inappropriate for children or adults. I don't like it."

He wrapped his arm around his new wife, pulling her close enough to kiss her cheek. "C'mon, babe. Tell us."

"Ugh. A farmworker from Mexico, Milagros, was murdered. All this creepy supernatural stuff happens, like Bloody Mary. You know what, you tell them, Belinda."

"It's true. Milagros was on this very farm. This house is where the owners lived like gilded folk while the farm workers had to endure terrible conditions for shit pay. She was planning to leave but never made it past that road just beyond the house."

An event horizon in the middle of Texas.

★   ★   ★

As Milagros tried to sleep, a new beginning was all she could think of. The conversation with Guadalupe and her family gave her joy, something she hadn't felt in a while, and she wouldn't have to travel to California alone. Perhaps this future would include love. That night, she turned in early so she could be at the post office as it opened its doors, followed by a full day of work. The excitement and anxiety of change caused her body to flop like a fish on a hook on the uncomfortable mattress. There were plans within plans that were waiting for her out *there*. So much for sleep. Milagros had enough of her own obsessive thoughts and the smelly overcrowded accommodation. She tossed the bandana on her bed and left without looking back or taking anything with her.

Behind the camp lay scrubland where she would sit against a large ceiba tree while listening to the chicharras sing her to sleep. Besides home, this was her favorite spot. The monotonous tone was a white noise that distracted her from the ache of the day's work, relentless worry about her family, and the unanswered question of how much of this migrant life she could endure. Not anymore. "La Causa," she whispered to the tree.

She settled at the base of the trunk, allowing her head to lean back to give her a view of the clear night sky and full moon. The distant stars could be home to anyone. A soft coo above her head and reflective owl eyes made her smile. Nocturnal creatures eased her loneliness because the language they spoke was universal. The flapping of wings, a scuttle of legs, even a distant howl of something that could probably eat her alive were all sounds she welcomed. They were all proof that things could thrive in the shadows. This gave her some hope. Her English was still a work in progress that she tried hard to perfect. Perhaps if she blended in, people would see her differently. Maybe she would feel differently about herself and have courage like that man in California.

When she could feel herself slipping into a dream, a familiar, nasal voice awakened her.

"If it isn't the spic bitch that thinks she is so damn beautiful. Always tryin' to get the attention of our men." It was Tanya and three of her friends. Milagros ignored them, thinking they would call her names, maybe spit on her, then leave. Abuse wasn't new and there was no use fighting something that no one cared enough to stop. It wasn't until they rushed at her that she knew something was terribly wrong.

The rope was an unanticipated burn, like hot oil popping from a frying pan, as two women pinned her to the tree by the neck. She thrashed with her arms and tried to kick one leg at a time, but the more she fought the deeper the rope dug into her throat. She had to swallow her cries as her voice was a broken thing, unable to carry. Tanya picked her up by the armpits so that Milagros was in a standing position. One of the women secured the rope that rested just below her chin with a tight knot on the opposite side of the tree. Milagros's fingers dug into the crevice between her neck and the rope, trying to catch a little slack so she might scream or breathe. She scratched so hard, a few fingernails nearly broke off. The skin around her neck was a shredded collar of blood.

"That's gonna leave a terrible scar!" Tanya giggled like a young girl playing tea party. The two women that tied her neck to the tree then bound her hands behind her back. Her fingertips scraped against the tree. "How did you know I was here?" she managed to rasp.

A smaller rope was used to tie her ankles together. She had no choice but to stand upright. Every movement was a fresh wound that left her feeling on the verge of falling unconscious. Tanya stood in front of Milagros.

"Billy keeps all sorts of things in the back of the truck. Whenever I saw that rope, I imagined how good it would feel to teach you a lesson. It was only by some strange stroke of luck me and the girls were out here drinking. We usually change spots to avoid gossip from the old folks when the boys are occupied by the ball game. I promise, you fuckin' spic bitch, none of our men will ever look at you again. Bring the buckets from the back of the truck, Janice. I just had an idea! Tiffany, go find a fire ant mound. Shouldn't be hard because they're everywhere."

The one called Tiffany giggled as she searched the ground. "Found one. And it's big."

The woman named Janice paused with two buckets in her hands. It was the woman Milagros had seen with the preacher. "You sure you want to do this, Tanya? That's enough now, she learned her lesson. Didn't you, you brown bitch?"

Milagros opened her mouth as wide as she could to capture every wisp of air that might keep her alive through this ordeal. She screamed for her sister in her mind, wondering if unbearable pain had the power to echo. She took mental snapshots of the women so that her sister might see. Every breath was a spark trying to light a match that could possibly reach someone – anyone – for help. What did she do to deserve any of this except show up to work and keep to herself? All she wanted was a better life. Why were her dreams rewarded with hate? But it was beyond hate. The fear manifests before the hate. Her bewilderment and sadness of an already hard life ending like this was erupting to rage. The rage was so great it felt like it possessed the power to swallow the sun and bring an end to everything. If only one of those stars would fall from the sky now. She wanted a rain of lava to burn this farm to the ground. Her belly growled in hunger to eat and digest their wicked hearts then shit them out to fertilize her own land, to reap rewards for her own and those like her. Did God see or hear? Where was he? Through tears she mouthed the word 'yes' to answer Janice's question. Milagros stared as best she could through the dark into the eyes of the woman who seemed to be hesitant about this prank.

In her spite, Tanya was not going to back down. "If you too chicken shit, *Janice,* then I'll do it." She snatched both of the buckets from Janice and held one of them out for Tiffany. She then turned her attention to Milagros, coming nose to nose with the bound woman, her eyes just as pale as Billy's, but narrower from the tightness of her ponytail and her inebriation. Milagros could smell the alcohol on her breath that could have easily been sulphur. She was so close even the tiny whiteheads in the creases around her nose were visible. Tiffany stood next to Tanya with a bucket teeming with fire ant dirt. Thin lips formed an air kiss as Tanya took the bucket from Tiffany, then dumped it over Milagros's head. Little legs and pincers cascaded down her body. Milagros tried to focus on the cicadas overhead, their hum, their song that always had the power to drown out everything that was bad. At first, the pain was a breeze brushing against her skin, until it turned to wildfire. The tiny beasts found every crack and crevice on her body to burrow into. Her veins no longer carried blood, only liquid torture.

The women all laughed except Janice, who stood there dumbly watching her feet as if trying to ignore the strangled cries coming from the woman on the tree. Tanya gathered cicada shells wild-eyed in the dirt.

Milagros felt herself seizing, as if she would forever become part of this tree. Hair, skin, nails and flesh morphed into solid bark of hate and anguish. Perhaps now they would cut her down and leave. Someone was bound to find her. Some of the older workers began picking before dawn to avoid the heat. Maybe she would have just enough strength to pull herself to the edge of the field. Ever so slowly the inside of her throat constricted, her lungs two deflated balloons with thousands of tiny pinpricks. Tanya approached her with another bucket.

"Here you go, beaner. Since we found you sitting with the dead cicadas, how about you eat them?"

"Can we stop this, Tanya? It's enough! I'm bored!"

Tanya ignored Janice's protestations, bringing her face close enough to kiss her friend. Then hitting the side of Janice's right leg with the bucket, causing her to recoil and wince in pain.. "If you don't shut the fuck up, I might go telling everyone who you're fucking behind your husband's back. And what would the preacher think of his saintly lamb doing something like this?"

★ ★ ★

Janice could detect a hiss in Tanya's voice that bordered on the demonic. Tanya's eyes looked like empty dark wells of all that was evil in the world. This was not a friend or a woman who stood before her. Janice walked away. She would find an excuse to come out this way in the morning to check on the girl if Tanya decided to leave her on that tree. She prayed to God Tanya would have a little mercy in her heart. Come to think of it, Tanya was never kind; even as a young girl, she enjoyed torturing vulnerable things. Even caught her smacking a baby they babysat once. Janice glanced back momentarily at the woman against the tree and the living blanket of ants devouring her slowly, her face ballooning. It was too violent to watch. And at this moment, Janice feared Tanya, feared what she might do to her if she intervened. Better try to help tomorrow.

Janice climbed briskly through the overgrown grass to appease her growing dread. There were noises all around she didn't recognize. The parting image of the woman was etched into her corneas. Clouds floated over the light of the moon and stars, stealing the little illumination that guided her to the truck. She walked faster, ignoring her stinging legs as bushes and nettles scraped deep into her flesh. Then all the hair on her body rose. It felt like someone lingered behind her, ready to strike. The clouds shifted again, allowing her truck to come into view. Something flew past her face, scratching her forehead as it dipped in flight. She screamed and ran as hard as her legs would move until she reached her vehicle. Without hesitation she jumped into the driver's seat then locked all the doors. With the headlights on, she could see an owl flying towards the tree. She craned her neck to reverse. A face stared at her through the rear window for just a second, but it was enough to cause her to scream until her voice box ignited in painful flames.

It was the bloody grimace of a woman with eyes like an oil slick that threatened to pull Janice to a place where she would never find peace or escape. Worse than that, Janice had the feeling the creature *knew* what she had done. Chunks of muscle on the skinless countenance twitched, bulging veins and capillaries throbbed like larvae. Yet her hair fell smoothly past her shoulders with the sheen of a black cat. The window fogged from the creature's hot breath as a thin tongue licked the glass. Then it was gone within a blink. Janice pulled away from the field, not caring if she damaged the car as the wheels screeched and sprayed dirt in every direction. She prayed for a miracle to erase this night from her mind as she reached the main road, but she was happy she made the wise decision to leave that unfolding nightmare at the tree.

★   ★   ★

Tanya shoved a handful of cicada shells into Milagros's mouth before gagging her with a red handkerchief. Milagros's throat was as tight as her panic as it continued to swell, leaving her lightheaded as she struggled to breathe. The little moisture left in her mouth was absorbed by dry cicada bodies stuck at the back of her throat.

Tanya held up a compact mirror to Milagros's face. "Not so fucking pretty at all."

Milagros could only see shadow through puffy eyes, but what she could make out was a reflection she didn't recognize. Large, circular red welts from the ant bites deformed her features. Blood oozed from beneath the rope around her neck. She closed one eye, not wanting to believe this was her fate. So close to sprouting wings.

Milagros didn't notice when the women left, without bothering to untie her. The hum of cicadas was a symphony in her ears as small legs scuttled across her scalp and shoulders. Miniscule mouths kissed her flesh. It couldn't be more ants because there was no longer any pain, only song. The chicharras formed a cocoon to take away her agony as they removed the venom from the ant bites. Relief at last. She gave in to their lullaby, trying to picture her home in Mexico, her sister's laughter, her mother's cooking, the songs they were taught as small children that felt more like spells than nursery rhymes – why couldn't she remember a single word when she needed them most? Mariposa kneeling in church and the natural curl of her eyelashes, butterfly wings. Her kisses just as soft. Lastly, she remembered that tearful goodbye filled with excitement at the prospect of making a bit of money for her family in the United States, making something of herself that wasn't dependant on a gold band. A small chicharra rested in the crook of her neck, its fluttering wings brushing her cheek and its song in her ear as she fell into a forever sleep.

I will see you soon, my daughter. We have so much work to do. Your power will not be wasted. You are the embodiment of their hate and they shall choke on it. It was the same voice in the wind from earlier that day. Why didn't her guardian angel help her win this fight?

Milagros's dead body was found at dawn.

*　　*　　*

The dining table was silent when I finished my story. Veronica had tears in her eyes as she still held Stewart's hand. The white guests could not hide their discomfort.

Stewart, being the nice guy, cleared his throat. "And that concludes the entertainment portion of the wedding." The table laughed and resumed their small talk.

"Sorry," I said.

Veronica gave me a smile. "I asked. Don't apologize. But let us agree never to talk about that again. Things are different now."

Someone said, "Absolutely."

This was her day, so I let it go. But something inside of me didn't want to let it go. I washed these thoughts down with another refill of my champagne glass. *Mind your manners. Be the fun girl*, I told myself. *Just get through another day.*

As I watched Veronica and Stewart leave, I thought of them walking the white beaches of Turks and Caicos followed by sweaty sex every afternoon. I wanted to feel loved whether that meant for the night or a few years. Conveniently, I'd often forget the restlessness I wrestled with when it came to male companionship. I'd ignore little things that were not exactly right until those little things either grated on my nerves like a tick digging beneath my skin, sucking and sucking away, or those things hurt so bad I feared my heart would collapse in on itself as I cried into a mascara-stained pillow. I've always liked new things since I was a child, although I never had many new things. There is also that initial crackle of electricity when you meet someone new that is euphoric, until that newness wears off. That bad habit always had a way of creeping up on me. Everyone said their goodbyes to each other, promising to stay in touch through whatever social media accounts they used most frequently. I was the last one to leave.

My body melted into a rocking chair while I listened to the

chicharras sing their song. With my eyes closed, the sun bore a hole through my forehead like it was creating a third eye. The Texas sun always felt good to me when coming out of the long East Coast winters. The bottomless mimosas rocked me to sleep until the last thing I remembered was the clanging of the champagne flute falling from my red manicured hand.

★   ★   ★

In my dream I was in the second-floor bathroom, except the bathroom was as it must have been years ago. Soft light penetrated a frosted glass window that was no longer there. I could see nothing but my shaded, haggard silhouette and the bathtub behind me in the mirror. A sharp point pierced the curtain. The sound of a slow rip pricked my ears as something effortlessly glided through the thin material. My heart pounded within my chest as I watched the tear become bigger. It was as if something was about to be birthed into our world through some perfectly formed slit in space and time. Whatever it was took its time creating a hole big enough to burst through. I couldn't move with the sensation of sleep paralysis holding my body still, but I couldn't look away either.

Then she came into view. Her flayed face was all muscle and blood, with eyelashes as thick as moth wings above completely black eyes that resembled shiny obsidian mirrors. A string of jade stones hung around her neck, covering the lobules, ducts and fat of her breasts. Beads of milk clung to her nipples. Her face and torso were followed by a distended belly. Through separated muscles I could see her uterus filled with amniotic fluid. A child floated weightlessly asleep inside of her, sucking its thumb.

A voice so tender but full of rage scratched at my eardrums. "Feed her."

★   ★   ★

I awoke to a sky of pink and orange sherbet sinking below the blue. My throat was so dry I could have been guzzling dirt instead of champagne all morning. The stabbing sensation of heartburn sat between my stomach and breastbone, a true sign I was drinking way too much. I ventured inside for water and Tums. There would be no more alcohol.

Hector sat on the sofa, looking at a photo album, when I entered the house. "You've been out for a long time." He motioned for me to sit next to him.

I grabbed one of the water bottles neatly lining a credenza at the entrance. My thirst was satiated for the time being. "What you got there?"

"It's my family. All this La Reina talk has me thinking more and more of my grandmother. My family is from Catemaco, Mexico. It's known for its beauty and as a center for witchcraft, or more accurately, its sorcerers. My grandparents started with one little market stall that turned into a shop, and now my parents own a string of botánicas selling everything you might need for life or magic. I lived there until I went to Harvard for business school…. The disappointment on their faces when I got that letter of acceptance. Not that they weren't proud of me, but the family business needed an heir. My sister was much more into all that supernatural stuff anyway. I told them to give her everything."

I sat next to him, smiling at the photos of children at play near a lake, all of them excited to be there except one. A man had a hand on the unhappy child's shoulder. I pointed to the photo. "You?"

Hector nodded and chuckled. "That would be me with my dad, a 'very powerful' – whatever that means – curandero. Since I was a boy, I've been told about the ways of curandismo in past generations in my family."

He flipped the page and tapped on a black-and-white photo of a woman by the same lake, leaning against a tree, barefoot, smoking a cigarette. She looked away from the camera with a relaxed expression. One hand slightly pulled up the hem of her dress.

"I don't want to believe any of it, except sometimes I'm visited by my grandmother. She seems to speak to me in my dreams. I don't know why, but I listen, and at times obey. I stopped trying to talk to my grandmother when she told me I would have a child. When Tom left, I couldn't see another way. God, I was so heartbroken. Still am in some ways. I didn't want to hear her voice. But I don't have the power to *not* hear her either." He closed the photo album. "You probably think I'm full of shit."

I told Hector about my dream. I didn't think he was full of shit, just superstitious, and probably lonely. Hell, I was ready to jump him before I learned that I was not his type. I was feeling so alone, desperate for a single touch to remind me I'm not a ghost just yet. Loneliness and misery are themselves curses. "How about we go look where it happened." Hector seemed happy to put away his memories that left a bittersweet smile on his face. I still had a few hours before my red-eye flight. I quickly changed into jeans and sneakers.

*   *   *

We walked for about fifteen minutes through dry, overgrown brown and yellow weeds until we stopped in front of a giant ceiba tree. The sound of insects was louder on the approach, then silent when we were just below its branches. The patch of parched soil surrounding the tree was littered with chicharra shells and nothing else. The grass as far as I could see resembled jaundiced skin. The only thing that appeared to have any remaining health or life was the tree and the creatures that scurried nearby.

"Here's the spot." Hector placed his hand on the trunk that was scarred from people carving their names in its bark. The words 'La Reina de Las Chicharras' were crudely cut and looked like the title of a slasher film. This angered me, the dismissiveness of it all. Her memory was not of her as a victim or a woman, but as a horror. My hands scraped against the bark as if I hoped remnants of her could be felt. I felt like a real asshole feeling sorry for myself, considering I had lived more life than her and the life she did live was infinitely more difficult. There was nothing here with her real name. I squeezed my eyes shut, picturing the scene. My heart filled with grief for the woman on the tree.

CHAPTER FOUR

Guadalupe rubbed her eyes once, still groggy from sleep. She'd stayed up late with her father and brother discussing their journey to California. That morning she wanted to fill Milagros in with their plan. Milagros wasn't in her bunk; only a discarded bandana lay in her spot. Guadalupe didn't ask anyone else because they groaned with the light entering the doorway. She knew sometimes Milagros stayed in the back field to be alone. Still no sign of her at the toilets or anywhere else. She would go to the place Milagros had confided to her.

In the distance, Guadalupe noticed a bulky shape attached to a tree. The brightness of the sunrise behind the silhouette made it difficult to see even when she squinted her eyes and blocked the sun with her palm. The sounds of crickets and cicadas rose the closer she came to the tree. Guadalupe gasped when she could see the figure clearly. Just last night. It couldn't be. But she could recognize those boots and dungarees anywhere. Her open mouth wanted to scream as she fell to her knees, but the cry that caught in her throat was a clenched fist blocking the sound. The terror of the bloated corpse covered with crawling insects made her explode from the inside out. Why? Why her? Why bring anyone here then treat them worse than animals? Guadalupe looked to the broken yolk of the fucsia and orange sunrise because she could not bear the sight of the atrocity. There truly was no God. Then panic hit. What should she do? Who should she tell? Her father or brother? No. Leave them out of it because, knowing this cursed place, they would be blamed. Guadalupe lifted her eyes to see something moving on the body of Milagros. A small square of white by her pocket. Guadalupe wiped her face and tried to stop the hitching of her chest. She rose and tenuously stepped closer. One unsteady step in front of the other until she was close enough to see a piece of paper. Slowly she reached out a fearful hand. A cricket popped out of the pocket, making her jump and scream. Guadalupe snatched the paper before shoving it into her own. The white paper made her think of where she should go.

She ran straight to the preacher. The discovery would be better coming from a white man of standing rather than her, unable to speak English and working there illegally. She ran past the fields, the bunkhouses with workers eating outside or waiting for the bathrooms, past the main house and down the dirt road to the small white church she had only been to once, but the man there was kind enough and spoke some Spanish. Her insides pounded against her bones and skin. The leather strap of her straw hat cut into her throat as it flapped behind her. Without thought, and hoping by some miracle he would be there, she pushed the doors open.

★ ★ ★

Pastor Rich was always an early riser. When he was growing up on a farm in Kansas, it became habit. In the stillness of the front pew at the feet of Jesus was the place and time he had his best ideas for a sermon. He sat next to a hot mug of coffee, pencil and pad of paper in hand. '*Crown of Thorns*', was all he had written before a burst of light flooded the church. As he turned around he saw a young woman running down the middle aisle, her face bright red from what he imagined was running hard for a distance. Tears and snot ran down her face. He could only understand part of what she said in Spanish; however, he understood the fear in the woman's face. She crumpled to the ground, lifting her head to the cross that hung at the front of the vestibule. A bleak rancor radiated from her gaze. Rich kneeled to speak. "Are you okay?"

She did not look at him. Instead she muttered, "Muerte," to the cross before looking at him and rising to her feet.

"Dime," he pressed.

She shook her head and began to walk out. She stopped in front of the car outside the church. He nodded and ran back inside to grab his keys. Guadalupe stared at the ground shaking when he returned. Her mind's eye fixed on whatever she wanted to show him. Once the engine roared to life, she said, "Perkins Farm. My name is Guadalupe."

★   ★   ★

The sound of insects was always a background murmur around those parts, but as they clamored through tall, dry grass, the noise became deafening, with all variations of insect fluttering out of their way rising into the air like flocks of birds. They stopped before a large tree that was the epicenter of the chittering of insects. The young woman fell to her knees to pray in Spanish between sobs. She pulled out tufts of grass and weeds, pounded her fists against the earth. All Rich could do was stare and try to stop his entire body from plunging to the ground next to her. Every hair on his body pulled towards the heavens, trying to fly away like the insects to avoid being in this unholy place. His stomach dropped to his balls, pushing breakfast towards his esophagus. He wanted to be sick.

The papers covered news about the lynching of colored folks in other parts of the country, unrest and such. You think in your mind it's wrong but then you turn the page, not wanting to subject yourself to such animosity. He never expected murder here, or to see something he couldn't flip past. This was a real person on this tree, and a woman. The cruelty of the scene made him want to cry, but he also wanted to know what kind of evil lived in someone to carry out such an act. What would prompt such a horror? It was a small comfort that her dignity was intact, her body still fully dressed. His faith was wavering as of late; he was falling in love for the first time in his life with someone who was unavailable, and now this. Why did God put these two women in his life? In his heart he knew he would be forever haunted by both. He escorted the young, inconsolable worker named Guadalupe back to the main house of the farm to alert the owner, Ray Perkins, and call the police.

Betty Perkins opened the door with her usual smile, which most considered pure sunshine. There was nothing disagreeable about Betty. She was friends with everyone as long as they were friendly in return. Her figure was still that of a woman in her thirties despite being in her late fifties, and the gray in her hair only complemented her tanned skin and blue eyes.

"Good morning, preacher," she said jovially, until her eyes dipped to the young woman with swollen red eyes who stared at the floor sniffling. The sunshine she tried to exude eclipsed into the black of night without him saying a word about the crime. Maybe she could read the alarm on his face. There also wasn't a quick invitation in. Not time to ponder silly things.

"I'm sorry to disturb you so early, but we need to call the sheriff straight away. There's been a murder on your property."

She looked right through him, like she was part of a conversation in her mind, ignoring them both and the tragic news he had just imparted to her.

"Betty? May we come in? It's urgent." Pastor Rich didn't want to sound gruff, but he questioned her reaction.

"I'm sorry, yes, please. A murder? That's awful! Who is it? Hope no one we know. Call straight away!"

She turned her attention to the young woman. "You poor thing. How did this involve you? Let me give you some breakfast and a drink. Coffee, preacher?"

Betty was known as a perfect host, and even in the midst of this dire situation, she took on that role. Rich felt uncomfortable around Betty but didn't know why. "I don't think I can stomach coffee right now. Just the phone."

She guided the young woman and Pastor Rich to the kitchen, where the phone was located, then took food out of the fridge. A pie, juice, butter, jam, bacon and eggs. Then she moved to the cabinets for mugs and glasses. If the sheriff and his boys were coming, they would want coffee. Breakfast. She turned the heat high on the cast-iron skillet to fry the bacon quickly. The sound of sizzling meat began as a low hiss until the cracking and popping of blistering flesh filled the entire kitchen. When the edges began to curl, she tossed the slabs to the other side. Betty glanced back at Rich to see if he watched her. What did he know? What would they find? The sting of grease hitting her hand broke her growing anxiety. *Just cook, Betty*, she told herself. The bacon seemed done enough. She placed it on a plate. Two eggs cracked to cook in the fat. She glanced back again, but this time to the first witness of the crime. Betty wasn't worried about her. They knew better than to bite the hand that feeds them.

The young woman sat at the table with silent tears in her eyes, spilling over her round brown cheeks. Not a sound. Betty turned back to the eggs to scramble them quickly. A dash of salt and pepper. Large glass of juice as a nice gesture. That would do. She placed the plate of hot food and juice in front of the young woman.

"Go on and eat up. You'll feel better. Most probably better than that camp food." Guadalupe looked at the plate, gulping the saliva in her mouth, then glanced at Pastor Rich, who was still on the phone.

Betty folded her arms. "Now, don't be ungrateful, girl. Eat." The young woman looked at Betty, then the plate. With all her strength within her stony hands, she grabbed the fork. Slow bite by slow bite, she chewed and swallowed as Betty watched on.

"Good girl. See, not so difficult."

Pastor Rich hung up the phone. "Sheriff and the boys are on their way. Suppose they'll contact Jim, the coroner. I told them to send an ambulance for this young lady. Her name is Guadalupe. I want to make sure she's okay. She looks really shaken up. Reminds me of my uncle when he got back from the war, after seeing his friends die like that.... I think maybe Guadalupe knew the woman on the tree. I'll do my best to translate."

Betty made no expression. "I think that is unnecessary. Look at her eating just fine."

Pastor Rich looked at Guadalupe, eating tear-sodden eggs and bacon, struggling to swallow. Just the smell of the food and coffee was making his stomach turn after the sight of the body. "Well it's done. We'll wait on the porch. Shouldn't be long."

Betty had already returned to her duty to prepare to entertain the gang of law that would soon take over her home. Ray would be down any minute and want his breakfast, too. In the end, Guadalupe finished every bite and drank every drop before leaving the kitchen with Pastor Rich. Betty cleared the plate and looked at the counter, dissatisfied with the amount of pie that she had. Maybe there was time for a quick batch of biscuits.

★ ★ ★

On the porch, Pastor Rich watched Guadalupe closely. She looked like she wanted to vomit the breakfast, but knew she couldn't. The young woman, who wasn't more than twenty, would probably swallow the vomit before letting it spill from her lips. What made him sick was Betty's behavior, so cold and odd.

But maybe because he had seen the victim, he was more affected. His body shook with adrenaline pumping hard through his veins. There were sirens approaching. Finally, help.

Ray Perkins and his nephew Billy clamored down the stairs to all the noise. "What's going on, Betty?" Ray asked in an irritated tone, in jeans and an undershirt sloppily thrown on. Billy was already fully dressed with boots in hand.

Betty didn't bother to look up from her busy work. "There was some accident on the farm, I mean...murder. I'm fixin' food but you should go on out to the porch and talk to the preacher."

The entire farm was disturbed with the sound of barking dogs and raised voices, people not knowing where to go or what to do. Billy went straight to the fields, trying to get the workers to keep moving along as if they were blind cattle. If anyone stopped to gossip or try to sneak away, they would be let go immediately without pay. They needed to know this wasn't no charity, this was work. There were plenty of 'em waitin' too. Nothing was happening that was any of their concern. Terrible things happened in life and that was the way of it. He wanted the entire situation under control and over with so it could blow over without it leaking to the surrounding towns. This farm was his ticket to all his hopes and dreams, and he would be damned if one woman who didn't mean much to anyone took that away.

Two police cars arrived at the Perkins house, with Betty already setting up a spread fit for a post-church luncheon. Ray stood on the porch with his arms folded across his large belly, still disheveled from sleep. The pastor and Guadalupe stood next to him, pale and vacant-eyed. Both Pastor Rich and Guadalupe refused to go back to the crime scene and opted to recount events on the porch. After, Guadalupe was taken to the hospital to be treated for shock. It was time for Sheriff Don and another officer to see the victim as they waited for the coroner to finish his breakfast. Alice, Texas was not used to this kind of fuss.

"Well ain't she ugly," said Grady, a young officer. He kept his distance, hoping he wouldn't be the one to untie the body.

Sheriff Don already knew this would have to be kept as quiet as possible. The victim wasn't one of their own, but it could cause a lot of noise for their community. "Let's just get this done and over before word gets out. You hear? Grab the boys and look for anything that might tell us who did this. Grass is tall so look close."

There wasn't a shred of evidence around or on the body to even know where to begin looking for the perpetrator of this crime. Different-size footprints scattered in every direction because this was an open space free for anyone to walk through. No murder weapon could be found once they set up a perimeter. She was fully clothed, which was a relief. There was nothing to say this woman didn't die from some sort of natural causes by the look of her after being tied up. Stroke? Heart attack? No gunshot wound. No knife wound. The only obvious wounds appeared to be some sort of insect bites that covered her exposed skin. By the look of the texture of the dirt on the body, the sheriff guessed ants.

Someone might have done this as a cruel prank, not knowing she would die. Cicada shells covered the crown of her head and cascaded from a jaw that hung loose.

Sheriff Don had been on the police force for most of his adult life and never did he see a crime scene like this. Even if it did begin as a prank, it ended in death. If only she was just alive, they could have come to some sort of agreement. Now he had to put the time in an investigation and keeping it quiet. The farms relied on these workers. The sounds of the insects buzzed and rang in his ears, making it difficult to concentrate. He swatted away the gathering flies attracted to the decomposing meat. This happened in the other parts of the South, not here. He'd never met a Klan member in his life. That kind of nonsense would never be tolerated. Alice was a quiet, wholesome place with folks being here for generations. These families were tied to the land; it was theirs. No, whoever did this could not possibly be local. *They* brought this here. What else could explain it? Must have been one of their own men mad at having his advances ignored. Probably moved on by now. His sister-in-law was living out there in California and told them about a Mexican field worker trying to unionize these people. Making a lot of unwanted noise. Demanding things. What a joke. They weren't even American. How could he do that? Who did he think he was? Don didn't want any trouble like the far south and he definitely didn't want any trouble for the farms around here, with the workers getting big ideas. He knew all the farm families, broke bread with them in their homes. Nope. Neither he nor his men would stand for trouble coming from outsiders. They would keep an eye on anyone who didn't belong. Everyone had a place. They weren't here to breed or put down roots, just work. True, this was a heinous crime, but terrible things happened every day. Yes, it was wrong, but by the looks of it there wasn't much they could do without evidence. It would have to be just one of those cases that went nowhere. A car approached in the distance. Maybe the coroner, who was taking his sweet time. Sheriff Don knew that car. Fucking Henry from the paper. Who in the hell told him already? Probably someone at the hospital.

Henry Doyle parked his car behind the police vehicles, then approached the sheriff with his Brownie Hawkeye in hand but did not look at him. His eyes were fixed on the body.

"Holy God, Sheriff. What happened here?"

"Morning, Henry. My guess is this young lady didn't like the attention of another worker and he didn't like that one bit. He made her pay in the worst way. Probably gone by now."

"Is that what the evidence suggests?" Henry walked closer to the stiffening corpse. This was the first murder he'd ever encountered. Chicago, Memphis, New York had all this, not

Alice, Texas. This was a story. The biggest story he would cover to date.

"Henry, if I allow you to print anything or take a photo for your paper, that is what you will say. You hear me?" Sheriff Don gave him a stern look to enforce his point.

Henry understood all too well. At least it was something he could send off to a bigger paper, not that anyone would care, but maybe they would. This was a story he couldn't wait to print.

"Understood, Sheriff." Henry licked his dry lips and approached the tree, focusing on the body. "Smile," he whispered with a snicker.

★   ★   ★

A distant voice. "Belinda, should we head back?"

I turned to Hector, who was speaking to me. "Her grave. Where is her grave?"

"That's at the Baptist church I'm surprised is still standing. The real estate agent showed me photos and it looked like it was ready to be bulldozed or abandoned." Hector paused and furrowed his brow. "Come to think of it, I've never been there... to her grave." He turned to the setting sun, which bled into the horizon with the darkness hovering above. The moon was just coming into view as a half circle.

"But it's going to be dark soon. You want to go to a graveyard at night? There are no streetlights around. The church has been there as long as this house."

If we were going to see Milagros, I wanted to pay my respects properly.

"You mind if I crash another night? Just tell me what I owe you."

He waved his hand for me to follow. "Your friend Veronica left a few bottles of Bordeaux that I wouldn't mind trying, and catering left my fridge full of food that I don't want to eat on my own. Of course, you can stay. This was my last wedding of the season before it gets too hot."

I canceled my flight, which I could easily rebook for the day after next. After, Hector and I settled in for life stories, two bottles of wine and leftover wedding food. When he stumbled upstairs, I could hear a doorknob twist and rattle. It sounded like he was ensuring the bathroom was locked.

The church was a short drive past a strip mall with a Hobby Lobby and Dollar Tree, down a two-lane road. Unlike those monstrous, shiny megachurches with big, flashing signage, this was a small wooden building with faded paint curling and flaking away. The roof needed repair, the shingles looking like a smoker's teeth.

We entered the graveyard. It was filled with grandiose oaks that shaded most of the graves. It was a relief from the sun, which felt like a fireball about to plummet to the earth. There was an elderly man with a faded trucker hat on his head and a white bandana secured beneath it, covering the back of his neck. He kneeled on a rolled-up towel, pulling weeds from around the graves with a small spade. It was so quiet you would have never known there would be a service later that morning.

He stopped his work as we approached. "Can I help you?" His eyes and eyebrows were almost a matching silver, both having lost their color with time. His crepe-paper skin looked like he had spent too much time in the sun in his long life.

"We've just come to see the grave of Milagros."

There was not a cloud in the sky, yet a shadow crossed his face. "Oh. That was a terrible, terrible thing. No one's been here for her. I'll show you myself. Just finished weeding that patch, so she's looking tidy."

The cicadas' song grew louder as we approached her grave. "You know anything about her?" I asked.

Shadow fled and memory took its place as he faced the sun. If only deep creases of time on one's face could predict the future like the lines of a hand. "I guess I can talk about it now. It was that young woman, Tanya, who did this. She and her friends who died. And the friends all died terrible deaths. One was pregnant." I saw a flash of shame in his eyes that he tried to disguise with this last piece of information.

"I can't believe she was never punished," I spat.

His eyes met mine. "You don't think lying in a hospital bed watching the world turn isn't punishment? She's still there. All her people dead, too. She's been moved to a home that isn't in the best condition. I go about once a month to pray with her. I need to believe she asked for forgiveness. I know it's selfish of me, but when you know the end is close.... Anyway, I don't know anything personally about Milagros, but I do have some boxes. I thought someone would claim them. Before Mrs. Perkins committed suicide, she brought over a ton of boxes for storage. You see, they were losing the farm and didn't know where they were going. She said it was personal records for when the time was right. She was on edge, seeing things. I did what I could for her, but it wasn't enough. She confided in me about the murder. I told her my conscience wouldn't allow me to know that information without taking action. I made it clear – she either told the police or I would. They were being pretty hard on the Mexicans and Black folks. May God forgive me. She killed herself not a day later. It was her letter of confession that revealed the truth about the murder, but it was too late for the police to do anything because they were all dead, except for Tanya. At the very same time I was at the police station, Tanya was on her way to the hospital. After that it all fell apart. The farm foreclosed and Ray moved to California to be with family with only the clothes on his back. No one wanted to touch the place, until this young man here decided to put all that money into it. Looks better than ever. Sometimes things just need a little love. Anyway, I'm not getting any younger and someone will have to clear this church out. Happy for you to look."

My interest was piqued. I wanted to know more about Mrs. Perkins and what she was experiencing. This part of the tale was not online. And I couldn't help but think about my dream. "What do you mean she was experiencing visions? Did she say anything specific?"

The old man lowered his eyes and shook his head. "I'll try to remember. Didn't make sense then and it still doesn't now. I honestly thought it was a dose of old-fashioned guilt."

CHAPTER FIVE

Alice Baptist Church, 1952

"Preacher, I need you to hear me. Please pray for me. Ask God for forgiveness on my behalf. I think the Devil is in my house and his demons are in my mind. They're creeping and crawling at all hours of the night! I can't sleep! Please, Preacher!"

"Okay, now, slow down. I know this is a hard time. That farm has been in your family for generations. They were some of the first to settle here, I understand. But God is with you. Keep your faith."

Betty and Pastor Rich held hands to pray in the front pew of the church. Betty resisted the urge to scratch her already torn, raw flesh, hoping some mighty power would fight the demons taking control of her life. She wished she had never heard Tanya and her nephew talking that night. Tanya came in later than usual, slamming the door behind her like it was her own home. The young woman always made it a point to go out with her friends on the days Billy wanted to be alone to enjoy watching his games with his Uncle Ray, but tonight Ray turned in early. Tanya giggled while rifling through the cupboards. Betty looked to see if Ray was going to be the one to tell her to keep it down; however, he remained asleep.

Betty threw the comforter across Ray's back and squirmed out of bed in a huff. She grabbed her bathrobe from the hook behind the door before making her way down the stairs to tell Tanya to shush and not leave a big mess for her to clean up in the morning.

One step lingered over the next when she heard the two talking. There was a strange excitement in Tanya's voice. The last words past Tanya's lips were, "She better be dead."

Billy told her to shut her mouth and not speak of this, then: "She better not be dead!" There was a pause before moans could be heard.

Betty returned to her room, not wanting to believe the conversation. Maybe it was a joke. She lay in bed with the stiffness of a mummy, eyes wide, with the comforter pulled to her chin as she stared at the ceiling fan. The following morning when the preacher showed up at the door with terror on his face, she knew it wasn't just talk. Why did she have to carry this burden? Betty chose not to tell the police Tanya was responsible for the murder. Why should everything they had worked so hard for be put in jeopardy? Why should a nice girl suffer for a stupid schoolgirl mistake? Betty had gone to school with Tanya's mother. They were decent folks. Betty had to believe it was all one big mistake. Tanya would never mean to do something so horrible.

But all that was for nothing, because they would lose everything anyway.

Then came the torment; the nights of sweating and scratching to the point she wished she could be a body without skin, a flayed woman, for just a moment, to enjoy some relief. It wasn't just the sensation of wanting to claw at her skin and scalp all night; it was also the visions when she closed her eyes. She could see microscopic translucent eggs nestled within her pores, ready to burst at any moment, releasing ants, spiders, silverfish and roaches. Worms slithered between her toes and lice hacked at the roots of her scalp. She wasn't wearing a hat for vanity these days; she was missing chunks of hair she'd managed to pull out as she slept. The Devil and God must be in league to make her pay. How much longer she could endure this test, she did not know.

That was when she decided to speak to the preacher. Perhaps he could help. She confessed all, showing him her patchy scalp, arms and legs. Betty wasn't expecting an ultimatum. At first, she was angry at him, betraying his own, but it made sense; he was a man of God. Could this provide salvation? Yes. Who knew what would happen next? She would give Preacher as many of the documents pertaining to the less legal workings of the farm she could squirrel away. Her husband wouldn't need to know. She returned home feeling better. The confession to Preacher gave her the energy to collect the necessary legal paperwork and write a letter detailing what she knew about the conversation she'd overheard between Tanya and Billy. She exhaled a deep breath when she put the pen down. She placed the letter and the paperwork in a plain box then wrapped it with brown paper. In large black letters she wrote, *For Pastor Rich*. She glanced at her watch. Still time before she would need to get supper started. She jumped into her car to head back to the church. With the engine still running, she stared at the steeple. She couldn't face Preacher again. His car remained parked in the front. She killed the engine then grabbed the box from the passenger's seat. His car would be unlocked. No one would ever steal from a man of God around here, not even the workers. She placed the box on the floor of the front seat. She exhaled again as she shut the car door. Time to go home for a hot bath. It would be in God's hands.

The bath, filled with fresh, clear, warm water, reminded her of the day she was first baptized at ten years old around a congregation speaking in tongues. This would be a baptism of sorts. Her reflection in the bathroom mirror was more horror picture show than the woman she thought she was. She began to cry. Instead of tears, maggots squirmed from her eyes. Their fat bodies plopped into the sink and down the drain. Her scalp itched again; lice eggs caked beneath her fingernails and coated her shoulders like dandruff. She looked down, feeling a burning sensation between her legs. Pubic lice coated the sparse untamed fur left at this age.

"No, no! It'll be fixed. Stop!" she whimpered as her hands clutched her face and scalp.

When she glanced at the mirror again, a figure lay just beneath the water in the bathtub. Betty couldn't move or scream upon the sight of the most terrible thing she had ever seen as the body rose, torso first, then turned its head towards her. It had to be a demon. God Almighty would never permit something like this to exist. She blinked, hoping the skinless, bloody woman in the mirror was just another waking nightmare. Betty knew it wasn't a nightmare when the woman grabbed her by the throat from behind. The flayed woman smelled like freshly cut grass after the rain and a hint of cinnamon. Water dripped from her body onto Betty, soaking her with pink wet tendrils. A string of jade and turqoise stones hung around the woman's neck. Betty could hear the woman's heart beating slowly, but there was the faint sound of another, much faster. It was coming from the belly of the woman.

"You will drink this, and you will die. My darling baby, Milagros, needs to be fed, and only your soul will do."

"Am I going to hell? You the Devil's slut to take me there?"

The flayed woman moved closer, sticking the tip of her sharpened nail in between two ribs. "I am the Queen of the Dead and my name is Mictecacíhuatl. Speak to me like that again and I will make this more painful than your human brain can even imagine. Why ask me of hell? What is hell? I've never seen it. I've heard of it but only on this world. Nowhere else in the many universes does it exist. I have come to believe this planet is the realm of hell. You want to believe in it so much, you have created it for yourselves. I am just a mother seeking nourishment for her child. And I am from Mictlan, a place of beauty and darkness."

"What will happen to me...when I die?"

The Queen brought the bottle of insecticide to Betty's lips.

"Drink and find out. Just as everyone's journey is different in life, so it is in death. It is futile to fight me. Surrender to your sins, because I will take you whether you like it or not."

"I deserve this, I know." Betty allowed her body to lean into the woman as she brought her lips to the bottle. There was no escaping this demon or the fate that awaited the farm. She sobbed quietly with the opening of the bottle resting on her bottom lip. The taste was acrid, the salt of her tears washing it away. The only emotion in her heart was guilt, for what she knew and what she wanted. She wanted the emotional agony to end, no worries about the farm, no physical torment. Without wasting any more time, she gulped the bitter liquid that caused her to heave. The Queen of the Dead placed her hand around Betty's mouth to prevent the poison from escaping. Betty dropped the bottle and clutched her throat. She couldn't breathe. Her esophagus burned with hell's fire while her legs lost control. And then there was nothing.

The Queen watched Betty convulse on the floor with a bloody foam oozing from her mouth. As Betty died, the Queen placed her hand on her lower belly, feeling it swell. She smiled, knowing her baby, Milagros, was satisfied. She began to sing in a soothing tone, "La Reina de Las Chicharras chicharrachicharrachicharra."

*   *   *

I wanted to look through the storage room even if it was a bunch of old paper we would chuck in the recycling. Hector thought there might be photographs he could use in the house or other remnants that might be useful. The back room of the church was a sweltering tomb of paper, smelling of dust and mold, spiderwebs blanketing everything. Silverfish scurried from underneath the boxes as we shifted them around, our lungs revolting in coughing fits from the room's contents.

"Those in back," the old man shouted between sips from a bottle of Coke as he sat in the pews behind us.

We brought the boxes into the main part of the church, which felt cool from the air conditioning. I hoped God looked down upon us and would guide us to who Milagros was. Maybe she had family somewhere. As I suspected, there wasn't much but ledgers on cotton and booze, books that didn't have much meaning anymore.

It was late in the afternoon when I came upon a box of handwritten documents with a different penmanship and photos. Most of the photos were of the family while the farm flourished. Then by some chance there was a notebook labeled *Domestic Help and Undocumented* that listed workers with their names, ages and where they were from. In ink that was nearly too faint to read, I saw *Milagros Santos – Undocumented female*. We knew where we could start. There were also old newspaper clippings. On the front page was the photo of a dead Milagros on the tree with people on either side of her body. They stood next to her as if she were a dead trophy animal instead of a murdered human. It reminded me of the migrant bodies washed up in Europe, and more recently other bodies in the Rio Grande river, a mother and child. I wanted to cry, to rip the paper in half at what they did to Milagros. In my heart I could feel a wicked desire to see the woman in the hospital and pull her life support out in front of her eyes. I would whisper, "This is for Milagros, you cunt."

I took the clipping with me and burned it in the sink of the church kitchen with a lighter I found in a drawer. That photo was never meant to exist. I needed to do something. I watched it burn through the name of the man who wrote the article and took the photo. *Henry Doyle.* I hope he burned too.

★   ★   ★

Henry returned home still early in the day to start his article and develop the photos. He was eager to get this out the door the same day. News like this couldn't wait. This was *his* story. Sheriff Don made the narrative clear. There would be no need to ask around the camp about the young woman or possible suspects. Just a short piece with just enough fear to keep people locking their doors and looking behind their backs. When you planted that first seed, readers would come back to see if there were any new twists in the story. This photo would surely shock. Henry began the process of developing the photos in his bathroom before starting the article. Between multiple drafts and the time required to develop the photos, the entire day went by fast.

The small bathroom doubled as a developing lab as it was easier and cheaper than venturing to a bigger town. Henry quite liked the solitude of it. When he developed photos beneath the red glow was when he got his best writing ideas. The room was dark and quiet as he watched the photo of murder turn to an image that could hardly capture the grotesque nature of the scene. Who knew what had happened to the young woman? It concerned him little; this would never happen to him or someone he knew. Look at the case of the Black Dahlia in 1947. She was a girl looking for trouble and found it, but what a sensation it caused. Maybe. this would be *his* Dahlia. But there were two main differences: the Black Dahlia was pretty and white, and it was a 'stars in her eyes' story. But it didn't hurt to try with what he had. It was still morbid. He left the rest of the photos to develop and walked to the main room with the developing chemicals he would leave in the sink for the time being. He placed the completed headline with the photo in a manila envelope ready to post to the editor in San Antonio. Alice was not large enough to warrant its own press, so they had a deal for a small local paper with the company that published the *San Antonio Express News*.

The sound of running water could be heard coming from

behind the closed bathroom door as he readied himself to leave. He put down the folder to have a look. He could swear he didn't turn it on, certainly not when developing photos. He opened the door and saw the water running at the maximum flow. The bathtub was nearly filled, threatening to spill over onto the floor. He turned off the water, glancing around in confusion. He unplugged the tub and turned towards the door to grab the folder and make it to the post office before it closed. He would grab dinner out tonight to celebrate.

★   ★   ★

The excitement of the day and three beers at dinner sent him to bed early that night. His deep sleep was disturbed by a single drop, followed by another, then a gush of running water. Henry thought it was a dream until it persisted. Then his bladder cramped, and he needed to relieve himself. He reached to the bedside table for his glasses. They weren't there. His vision was so poor everything appeared a blur, including the silhouette in front of his bed.

"Who's there? I don't have money or anything of worth. Take what's in my wallet if you must and the car keys are on the dining table."

The fuzzy shadow didn't move, then it was gone. He rubbed his eyes and blinked. The water was still running. He set his feet on the cold hardwood floor and peered towards the bathroom. The shadow stood in front of the door. He blinked again, feeling the sleep in his eyes become a sticky, scratchy goo. His eyelashes tore from the lids the harder he tried to open them. He ran to the kitchen sink to splash his face with water. He could barely make out the tap. Instinctually, he thrust his hands into the sink to catch the water. He'd forgotten a basin of developing chemicals lay at the bottom. A mixture of chemicals and water bathed his eyes. The burning was worse than the time he touched a hot baking sheet of cookies. He clutched his eyes, screaming from the fire eating away at his pupils. The neighbor must have heard his cries because there was a banging followed by a woman calling his name. Henry had lived in this apartment for years; he could navigate blindfolded. He opened it to Myrna.

"Oh, Jesus, Henry! Oh my God!"

"Call for help! There's someone here! I can't see!"

The single woman in her forties ran to her apartment. He could hear her frantic voice on the phone with someone, most likely the ambulance service. There was nothing but darkness. His face was going numb from the torrid pain, as was his mind, which focused on the person at the foot of his bed. Who was in his apartment? He did notice the water had stopped. But there were footsteps nearing him. "Myrna? Is that you?"

A faint hint of cinnamon and smoky chocolate filled his nostrils. "No, it is not, and you will not profit from death. Death is *my* domain." A wet hand grabbed his chin and cheeks, squeezing hard. He could feel his lips puckering to the shape of an *O*. With a forceful thrust, the hand threw his head to the side. "You act like a blind fool, then you shall *be* a blind fool. La Reina de Las Chicharras. Write about *that*." The female voice was low, almost seductive if not for all the anger he could detect.

He suddenly knew what this was about. The ghost of the murdered girl, it had to be.

"Myrna! Myrna!" He thought he would have to shout until he went hoarse, but he could hear her slippers pattering towards the open door.

"They're on their way! Are you bleeding now? There's blood on your face!"

"I need you to do something for me. I need you to call Donald Johnson at the *San Antonio Express News*. Tell him not to run the story I sent him. Please! As soon as it hits ten a.m.! He's in his morning meetings until then."

"Okay. I will. Just hold tight, everything will be fine."

Henry never recovered his full vision and the photo was published in the local paper.

★   ★   ★

I didn't have a job, had a decent severance package and alimony checks, so a little vacation to Mexico to bring closure to Milagros's family could be in the cards. There was nothing to return to except my two-bedroom condo, with one room being mostly an empty reminder of the child who was moving on from me. I didn't want to go home, or rather the place where I slept, but I didn't want to overstay my welcome with Hector. The probability of Milagros's family still living at that same address was pretty low, but at least the idea felt like a positive action in the world instead of my continual, narcissistic negative spiral. It was a long shot, but so are many things in life.

Hector and I loaded his car with the boxes for recycling and a single box of documents we wanted to keep. We returned to the church to say goodbye to Pastor Rich, who felt as lonely and forgotten as the church.

"Thank you, Pastor Rich, for allowing us to tear apart your storage and take a few things."

He hadn't moved much from his spot on the pew. "You're doing me a favor taking some of it away. I'm always here if you need anything."

"Tell me. What happened after she was found? How did she end up here?"

He wrung his hands while looking at the chipped, splintered cross that was just as age-ravaged as the statue of Christ hanging limply on the cross. His eyes were just as devoid of hope as those of the wooden Christ. "Let me rewind a bit. Start at the day of the untethering from that tree."

⋆   ⋆   ⋆

The bumpy ride back to the farm from the hospital barely registered to a numb Guadalupe. Her stomach felt empty after vomiting the breakfast she'd been forced to eat. She'd hated eggs since she was a child. Milagros had been taken from this world in a way Guadalupe would never forget. When Guadalupe kneeled before the cross after bursting into the church, she told Jesus he was dead to her unless he sent a sign. And quick. Sodom and Gomorrah-style vengeance. This place was worse. What a useless deity he was if he stood idly by. In that moment she wanted to rebuke her faith and sacrifice Billy to the heavens. It had to have been him.

Once at the empty camp, she ran straight to the shanty she shared with her father and brother. To her surprise, they were there. "I thought you would be in the fields!" she screamed, and began to cry into her father's chest.

"No. We stayed back because we couldn't find you! Some said there was a dead girl. We tried to ask questions about what had happened, but Billy told us to leave the farm. He gave us a day.. We are leaving for California, now."

Guadalupe pulled out a piece of paper from her pocket before crying again, her insides ripping anew. Pangs of pain radiated from her heart. "I found her. She will never leave me. Milagros is dead."

Her father held her tightly. She could hear him sniff and wet drops fell upon her shoulder. "Come. We go now. I've packed everything already. We will honor her in La Causa. Our struggle is still her struggle. For now, we must leave this cursed land."

Guadalupe kept that letter until her dying day and read it every year on the day of Milagros's passing. On Dia de Los Muertos, the letter sat in the center of candles with the bowl of the same caldo they shared, a recipe handed down for generations. The last supper. Only the freshest chrysanthemums without bruise were allowed on the altar for Milagros. She prayed that Milagros would be reunited with her loved ones and find a place of peace. Guadalupe also prayed for a day of reckoning.

★   ★   ★

The workers pulled together a small collection to give Milagros a proper burial, as she had no family. The one person she had been seen with, Guadalupe, left with her family in the chaos. Not a soul knew where or who Milagros's people were in Mexico. The newly appointed local Southern Baptist preacher, Pastor Rich, agreed to bury her body in his cemetery because, despite being a Catholic, she was still a child of God. He decided to hold the service outside so they could bring in extra chairs for the workers. His sermon was an angry, impassioned rant with parts said in the little Spanish he knew.

Pastor Rich couldn't recall so much sweat and spittle ever flowing from his body. The Holy Spirit made itself known when he needed it most. Afterwards, he made it a point to shake the hands of all the workers, trying to persuade them to stay for sweet tea. They were honest working folks who helped out during the war when the rest of the boys were fighting those Nazis. The Bracero program aided his own family when they struggled to keep up their farm in Kansas. The workers never gave his family or anyone trouble. Sure, every now again they would fight amongst themselves, but people were allowed to disagree. His own brother wanted to take swings at him for following God instead of his duty to his family. Now he watched the workers shuffle away, hats in hand, speaking amongst themselves with sagging shoulders as the rest of the flock gathered elsewhere. They were clearly not welcome after bringing such a perceived disgrace to the town. But he couldn't get the image of the dead young woman out of his head. He would say a quiet prayer for her soul whenever her bruised face would cross his thoughts, because this thing that happened wasn't just a disagreement or lust. This was far worse, and scared him more than the thought of the Devil.

*　　*　　*

A week passed before the farm returned to its usual everyday routine. All of Milagros's belongings were packed in a brown box by Billy and left in the front of the bunkhouse for people to take what they wanted. But no one dared touch or look in the brown cardboard box. It sat under the sun and rain until all the contents became one under mildew and dust. Then one day the box was disposed of by an unseen hand. Everyone was silently happy to see it gone. There was an unspoken sense that if you did take something, you might pay dearly later for dishonoring the dead. Milagros might even come back to retrieve her possessions. The rectangular spot where she had slept remained bare. No one wanted to sleep in the last place in the world where Milagros had laid her head. The fires that burned to the tune of the guitar now jumped with sparks from the whispers of the workers about the tragedy of Milagros. No one said it out loud; however, there was a sense she was not gone. Every screech and howl seemed to form the sound of her name. The fear of one of them being next soiled the hearts of every worker. No one wanted to be made an example of the way she had been. Their suffering would not be in body, but in silence.

It was a Sunday evening, exactly a week to the hour later, that the farm fell into the clutches of a curse not seen before.

Tiffany was first.

*　　*　　*

The thought of the Mexican woman was a stain on her memory that could not be scrubbed clean. She struggled to sleep after an officer, Grady Boone, her junior high crush, showed up on her doorstep in his tan uniform, which fit nicely on his lean body. A single dimple on the side of his cheek winked at her when she opened the door.

"It has been some years, Tiffany. May I come in?"

She looked away in shyness from her wanton heart. There was also that unrelenting nervousness that their crime would be discovered.

"Sure. What brings you here today? Not a date, I hope. You know I'm a married woman now." Charm. She would use her charm to hide her fear.

He stepped into the house, looking around until his eyes landed on a wedding photo. "Nothing really. Sheriff is tying up loose ends for the necessary paperwork before he officially closes the investigation. You spend a lot of time at the Perkins farm with Tanya. Just want to know if you heard anything. Tanya mentioned that you were all together since the men were occupied with the ball game."

A feeling of relief allowed her to enjoy this moment alone with her old flame, her first flame. The investigation would be closed. Prayers answered.

"I mean, we don't mix with the farm workers. Too many came through not even speaking English. Haven't heard anything from the domestics either. Sorry. A terrible thing to happen to a woman."

Grady and Tiffany stood in an awkward silence because she was no longer available, as much as they both wished she was. With nothing to keep him there and no signal telling him she wanted him to stay, he thought it best to leave.

"I guess I'll be going. Thank you."

"Anytime." Tiffany was disappointed to see him go, but it was for the best. Infidelity was a sin she didn't want to commit, and although it seemed the law wouldn't be giving them trouble, she still wanted reassurances from Tanya that no one was about to snitch. She set a time and date to meet Tanya as soon as Grady could be seen driving away.

*   *   *

The Perkins house always looked grand from whatever direction you approached it. It was a Victorian masterpiece in Texas, showing the locals what the American dream looked like. The single spire on the corner was straight out of tales of Cinderella or Rapunzel.

Tiffany parked at the edge of the property as instructed by the sign. The grass and flowerbeds were not to be tarnished by tire treads. Tanya answered the door with a goofy smile, her teeth clenching over her bottom lip. "Come on. Let's go talk in the barn," she said in a low voice, glancing back before stepping out and closing the door with as little sound as possible.

Tanya pulled Tiffany by the hand to the barn. As soon as they were alone, Tanya let out malicious laughter. Not a blush of shame or paranoia.

"Can you believe the fuss everyone is making over that girl? I listened to the whole thing at the top of the stairs. After the sheriff came back from seeing the bitch, he questioned us. I should be a Hollywood star by the way I told them tales of those dark men whistling and harassing me! But I was *too* scared to say anything. At least they think it's one of their own. A sex-mad Mexican!" Tanya grabbed at Tiffany's breasts with her tongue hanging from her mouth before folding over in a fit of red-faced laughter.

Tiffany tried to mask her horror at this reaction. The smell of horse manure turned her stomach. What did they do? There was actual pride, almost a sensual tone in Tanya's voice as she spoke of the act. The coldness in her eyes was a temperature that was not felt this far south, even on a winter's day. Tiffany couldn't see what lived behind Tanya's hard, dead eyes, but she knew Tanya was reliving every second like a picture show as she spoke of the way Milagros sputtered and gagged on the cicada shells in her desperation to breathe. It made Tiffany want to run in terror in case that bloodlust suddenly shifted to her. Why Tanya loved that no-good husband, who would fuck around with a discarded glove if he fancied it, was beyond Tiffany, but they had to stay with Tanya on this. They grew up together; they did this terrible thing together. "You sure no one's about to talk? Grady was over at mine two nights ago. But don't worry, I took care of him with the story we agreed on. Case will be closed."

Tanya stopped her laughter. A dead, flat expression matched her steely eyes. "Of course, the case is closed. Because we tell the stories for them. It's the way it has to be."

"Yeah, 'course. You're always right, Tanya. Anyway, I better go so I can make the supermarket before supper." Tiffany returned home, knowing she would take this secret to her death. She didn't need to go to the supermarket, but nothing could keep her alone with Tanya. Not to save her life.

★ ★ ★

After fidgeting and squirming around in bed to find a comfortable position while listening to the sound of her husband's snores, Tiffany decided to get up. It would be morning soon. She would sit on the porch with a cup of coffee and maybe watch the sunrise, and ask God for forgiveness. Thank Jesus they got away with it.

Tiffany slipped out of bed and walked quietly into the darkened kitchen. She had lived in that house for two years now and knew every corner without turning on a single light. Gordon hated being disturbed while he slept. The cupboards were meticulously organized, so she could cook an entire meal blindfolded with little to no noise. Gordon hated having his ball games disrupted by the clattering of pots and pans. As she waited for the coffee to percolate, she placed one foot in a slipper tucked beneath a chair. When she thrust the other foot into its slipper, she felt a hard pinch in the center of her foot. "Fuck!" she screamed, loud enough to probably rouse her husband. With one hand she covered her mouth while she tried to inspect the source of pain by lifting the injured foot. Momentarily her body wobbled as it tried to regain balance. She winced, bringing the foot higher to see the injury in the dim light. A shadow crossed the room. Thinking it was Gordon, she jerked her head up. The sudden movement threw her off-balance again. Another shadow. She stretched her head towards the first signs of gurgling, boiling water where the shadow moved. As she lowered her foot, heart palpitations quickened the pulsing veins in her neck. She lost all control of her legs in an instant. One arm pinwheeled, searching for anything to prevent a fall. Fingertips grazed the back of a chair before the base of her skull crashed against the edge of the thick wooden table made from the trees in that part of Texas, a wedding gift from her parents. A crack that reminded her of jointing a chicken filled her ears, followed by a ringing. She lay on the floor feeling a wave of warmth travel from her foot, to her leg, and continuing the length of her body. It could have been the first steps into a hot bath if not for the paralyzing effects seizing her muscles. The ringing became louder as her face went numb until it traveled to her throat, which was now a sinkhole of sand closing tightly around breath. The memory of Milagros trying to take her last gasps with one pleading eye that begged for mercy she did not receive veiled Tiffany's mind. Tiffany knew she was about to die. Something wet trickled against her face, like molasses oozing out of an overturned jar. Red liquid jam that surrounded her brain created a small creek on her linoleum floor. Breaths shortened, her head throbbed with the ringing. Eyelids began to sink, but before they shut, she saw the smallest brown spider crawl in front of her eyes into the puddle of her blood. It paused as if it meant to say, "Here I am," before continuing its journey, leaving bloody dots as it scuttled away. Tiffany Borden was dead within minutes.

Gordon slept through her initial scream and didn't stop howling in terror after he found his wife's body.

★   ★   ★

Tanya, Daisy and Janice clung to each other during the funeral, crying over the random, senseless death of their friend. Tanya remained silently confident despite her exaggerated, fake show of grief. One less set of loose lips. She made a mental note of how shaken Tiffany was when they talked in the barn. As she watched Tiffany leave that day, she thought a murdering pervert might have to return to shut her stupid trap. Lucky for her it didn't come to that. Tanya now watched her friend's body being lowered into the ground, the wails of her family filling the cemetery. She felt nothing but relief when the first shovel full of dirt was cast over her casket.

★   ★   ★

Only one day passed before another woman in the murdering pack also met her end.

Daisy Matthews sat at the table for supper with her parents, like she did most nights.

"It smells magical, Momma, as always," she said. Daisy scanned the table, feeling her hunger rumble. Biscuits smothered in a rich gravy with chicken-fried steak, mashed potatoes and fried okra lay in the middle of the table, the heat rising with the aroma of the freshly cooked meal. She inhaled deeply. As soon as "Amen" was said by her father, Abraham, Daisy greedily heaped her plate with the first helping of chicken and mash, her tongue between her teeth before anyone had a chance to get there first. This became habit when she'd had to fight for seconds against her five siblings growing up. Now, as the last to leave home, she had her parents all to herself. Daisy could eat as much as she wanted, as if she were an only child. To cheer her up after the awful events, Momma even made a pecan pie. Daisy felt terrible about Tiffany's death, couldn't stop crying when she found out, but in her heart, she loved all the fuss that was being made over her. People went out of their way to say hello and ask how she was doing. Even Gordon asked her to come over to help him pack away his deceased wife's clothing because he didn't have the heart to be so close to her scent. They shared a few beers and she could swear there was something in his eyes that wanted her to stay for one more. Momma and Daddy were making sure she had everything she needed before she even asked for it. It was a terrible thing her friend was gone, but this felt like a new life beginning for her, starting with that pecan pie right after supper.

Daisy lifted a forkful of potato and chicken to her mouth. A soft crunch was followed by something stringy moving against her palette. She stuck two fingers into her mouth to retrieve the foreign object. A large, winged cockroach with a smashed tail that oozed innards stared back at her. Its antennae twitched in confusion. She gasped, causing a leftover chunk of chicken-fried steak to lodge in her throat. She dropped the roach to clutch her neck, trying to gulp for air with undigested food twisting in her belly from fear. A memory of the woman on the tree unable to breathe and the way the moonlight illuminated her contorted death mask was all she could see. Daisy hadn't taken the time to think about the dead woman since that night. She was drunk and angry that Billy had moved his eye from her to this woman who was nothing but a dirty farmhand who didn't pay him no mind. How quickly he forgot the hand job she had given him not two weeks before in his truck as he drove her to work at the bowling alley. She missed the flutter of nerves when Billy would give her a wink or brush up against her behind Tanya's back. The excitement of a secret admirer was a small promise it wasn't too late for her, because there were very few available men her age left unmarried. The gall that he would find this raisin-colored bitch stinking of beans prettier than her fueled participation in the prank gone right that night. She wanted Milagros to suffer for taking away Billy's attention. Now she felt guilty.

Daisy squeezed her eyes shut and prayed, *Jesus, please!* She could feel her consciousness blinking on and off like a broken light bulb. She screamed in her mind so that the heavens would take notice. She promised God, if he saved her, she would never commit any more heinous sins and even go to the law to tell them it was Tanya who wanted to teach the young Mexican a lesson.

A vision of the woman on the tree, Milagros, was the only response Daisy received. The malformed, ant-bitten figure broke free from the ropes, howling in laughter at Daisy. Cockroaches with wings flew from her shoulder-length brown hair. Her open mouth spewed ants, crickets and worms with viscous blood dribbling down her chin as the laughter became louder, more maniacal, until Daisy feared her eardrums might burst. Gashed fingertips pointed at her. The laughter now took the form of words: "La Reina de Las Chicharras."

Abraham and Sally watched, thinking their daughter would eject whatever was caught in her throat. "Drink some of this," Abraham said with confidence as he slid his beer towards Daisy. He was sure the carbonation would wash it down or bring it up.

"Do something!" Sally screamed at her husband. She jumped from her seat, twisting her apron, unable to move any further from the shock of the moment. Daisy's face was changing color, her eyes not in the room but somewhere far off. It wasn't until her face went beet red that Abraham dashed behind his daughter to smack her hard against her back with a palm that stretched across her shoulder blades.

Every slap was a ray of hope for Daisy. Milagros continued to stare at her in the middle of Daisy's mind. She wiped the blood off her chin with the back of her hand and smirked. "Adios. And enjoy hell." She waved a hand of broken fingernails and continued to shriek with laughter.

Daisy's bloodshot eyes bulged before her face went purple and then cold blue. Daisy Matthews collapsed in her father's arms.

"Daisy. Daisy!" Abraham screamed, shaking his daughter's limp body.

The roach crawled along the table by its few remaining legs until it fell to the floor. It continued to crawl slowly on its belly across the floorboards and out of sight through a crack in the wall.

★   ★   ★

Texas thunderstorms can be sudden and violent. During one such storm the sky cracked loudly with peals of thunder, sounding like the universe itself was being shaken. Janice Pritchard and Tanya Peyton held fast to each other beneath an umbrella at Daisy's funeral. Neither wanted to admit something was very wrong since the night they murdered the Mexican woman, Milagros. They had finally learned her name.

Raindrops and tears wet their faces. The chill of the storm and fear made their legs shiver. Janice could admit she was part of a murder. But it wasn't just the two deaths in their little gang that startled her and added to her declining mental stability. Large patches of crop had withered without cause. Locusts ravaged the cotton, and what the locusts didn't eat, a fungus destroyed without pity. When Janice tried to sleep, the cicadas seemed to perch right against her window, whispering, "La Reina de Las Chicharras", over and over again, like the sound of a typewriter that never ceased to pound against her skull. At this point there would be encyclopedia-sized volumes of that name repeated without punctuation. Tanya showed no signs of worry or fear, which reminded Janice not to trust her. The tears Tanya cried were for one person only: herself.

★   ★   ★

After two days of torment and the previous night of no sleep, Janice shuffled in groggy awareness into the bathroom to splash water on her face, with the words 'La Reina de Las Chicharras' still on loop. Perhaps if she said them out loud, they would go away. Janice wanted to confess, anything to make that stupid Spanish name, or phrase, or whatever it was, go away. She stared in the mirror, dark circles beneath her eyes from this extended lack of sleep. Her middle-school acne returned from the stress of the secret she carried. Janice said the words, "La Reina de Las Chicharras", while looking at her reflection as she gripped the edge of the sink.

There was only silence until her skin began to feel like jumping hot popcorn just beneath the surface. The pustules of acne grew until they resembled swollen purple bites with tubes of pus oozing from the center. Her throat tightened; the itching caused her chest to hitch and she struggled to breathe. This left no room for screams to escape the horror in the mirror. Janice clawed at her neck as if she could release the invisible thing choking her. She wanted to turn and run, but her feet were solidly rooted to the ground, like that ceiba tree, or like in one of those dreams that you can't wake from where you lose the ability to move.

In the mirror, she could see a silhouette that wasn't there before behind the shower curtain. The curtain bulged; it was real. The silhouette became a solid body moving towards her. Piles of insects crawled from inside the bathtub, filling the room with their noise, and blanketed the floor. They surrounded her feet like an army overtaking an enemy. Janice tried to scream again, but no sound dared to exit her body as the shower curtain was nearly fully extended. She snapped her eyes shut. *I rebuke you in the name of Jesus!* she cried out in her mind. As if a spell had been broken, she breathed in and out through her nose.

When the chittering of insects stopped, she opened her eyes again. Everything was as it was before, except a note had been scrawled in blood on the mirror.

Jesus can't save you from me. I want to feed on your soul.

The fear of God and the Devil replaced Janice's exhaustion.

Without telling Tanya, Janice made up her mind to go to the police. She would also tell her husband she was sleeping with the new preacher pretty much ever since he arrived in town. After her third miscarriage, she'd sought spiritual guidance to rid herself of the bitterness and depression clouding her days. This new pastor had a way of looking at her like she mattered. The thoughts his touch gave her were anything but pious. She and the pastor had more in common than she had with Jay, at least now. They were so young when they'd decided to become a couple. After her third meeting with Pastor Rich she kissed him on an impulse as they held hands in prayer. His lips were impossible to ignore in the middle of asking for the Holy Spirit. Without hesitation he kissed her back, followed by passionate sex in the storage room.

Before the confession of her adultery, she would lay flowers at the ceiba tree and apologize, beg for forgiveness, because Milagros was still here reaping her revenge. Janice believed Milagros deserved to punish them, yet maybe Milagros would be forgiving. After all, Janice felt she didn't know what she was doing that night. Yes, she should have done more to stop the torture, but she was slightly drunk. Not that being drunk was an excuse, or hating the workers who worked for less than white folks was any reason to let someone die the way that young woman did. And when she examined her heart, she knew Milagros would die if she didn't intervene. Janice had to pay for thinking of her own skin before Milagros, who didn't deserve this horror in the slightest. Janice promised God, if he saved her from whatever was happening, she would be a better person no matter the consequences. In small towns like Alice, your penance was the shame felt as you walked past hushed voices recounting your sins.

★   ★   ★

Janice trudged to the tree at midday to prevent frightening herself, despite a daggered fear inside her bowels since the moment she opened her eyes in bed. Every death so far had occurred in the dark, so surely she was safe. The closer she came to the tree, the louder the insects got. Just like the night before in her bathroom. She stopped in the middle of the field, thinking perhaps she should run back home and hatch a plan to leave Alice, maybe even her husband, but there was nowhere to hide from this crime. She took a step forward and willed herself to keep moving until she reached the tree. She kneeled in front of the thick base to pray with a bouquet of the best roses from her garden.

With eyes closed, she prayed, "Milagros, I want to say I'm sorry and ask your forgiveness. I asked God for forgiveness, too. I promise to tell the police everything. I accept any punishment they see fit. Please spare me. Help me to be a better—" Mid-sentence, a sharp stab punctured her thigh. Then she heard the unmistakable sound of a rattle. She looked to her left to see a coiled rattlesnake watch her sway from the venom spreading from the bite to the rest of her body. She collapsed to the ground as it continued to shake its tail. It did not get any closer or strike again. It simply watched her cry. She turned her head towards the tree at the humming of the cicadas that infested her ears, vowing to never leave her alone.

"I said I was sorry! Why? Please! I think I might finally be pregnant!"

This wasn't a lie to garner sympathy. She still hadn't bled that month, and if she was with child, she didn't know who the father was. It was wrong, but she secretly wanted it to be Rich, the pastor who filled her with desire and blossoming love. Janice could feel her eyelids open and close like paper fans, her strength draining as the poison spread through her veins. She managed to raise herself to her hands and knees to crawl towards the fields, where she could be seen by the workers picking what was left of the cotton. Her chest tightened faster than she thought it would. Were snake bites that potent? Milagros must not have accepted her forgiveness and God didn't care; or he was giving her the Old Testament treatment of wrath for all her wickedness. With vision tunneling and all her will gone, she fell into a pile of soft white cotton, feeling her heart slow with every breath. She died to the hymn of cicadas chanting, "La Reina de Las Chicharras", and the workers calling for help in Spanish. The blue sky darkened as she wondered what hell would be like.

*   *   *

Tanya was now the only one left. Her guilt had become a coiled viper inside her belly, continually nipping at her day and night. The poison kept her vigilant. She paced around the house in a foul mood, scarcely speaking or eating and refusing to leave the house, claiming she was too filled with grief from losing her childhood friends to do anything. Not true. Tanya was afraid she would be next. For the first time, she felt afraid of her own reflection. The small noises of creaking floorboards and mice caused her to jump. She stopped peeling back the curtains to spy on the outside world. It was nothing but rot creeping over the abandoned farm and increasing numbers of cicadas claiming every spare inch on the exterior of the home. The racket was deafening.

Billy acted oblivious to it all. He focused on keeping his aunt and uncle in business, which meant he was only home when he had to be, but they wouldn't miss the funeral even if he had to drag her there by the ponytail. It would look bad. If things turned way south, he wanted to make a play to take over the farm for himself, and Tanya of course. This tragedy was one big inconvenience, but it could be the stroke of luck he needed to be the boss instead of the hand. There would be no one to keep him in check or tell him how to run things. Billy had ideas, so many grand ideas.

Tanya looked out the kitchen window only when Betty grew tired of the darkness in the house. The gross winged creatures would be there, beating against the glass. This churned her anger. The noise they made was an irritating reminder of that bitch. That bitch and all her kind.

"That damn Bracero program in '42. The whole of Texas, then the entire country will go to hell, just watch," Daddy would boom as he pulled off his worn work boots with calloused hands. Tanya missed Daddy. He would have known what to do. He might even still be here if he hadn't lost his job because of all the other workers piling in from all over but local. They said it was a heart attack. Daddy died working himself to an early grave because he had to. Thinking of her family's past plight made her rage inside. She relived the moment she dumped the bucket of ants on that bitch's head and felt good about it. She had no regrets. Tanya slammed her palm against the window to disturb the insects. Their wings and chittering continued more frenetically than before, ignoring her presence. She closed the drapes forcefully and walked away seething. Betty watched on like a phantom, not bothering to open them again.

★　　★　　★

The farm continued in restless disorganization. Many of the workers had already left for more fruitful pastures, leaving the remnants of viable crop going to the insects or decay. New workers refused to join, fearing whatever was cursing the farm would follow them. They'd heard about the murdered woman and the farm's slow demise. This was an old-fashioned curse. "Santa Muerte? How else can it be explained?" some whispered. Milagros had a new name, La Reina de Las Chicharras, because of the unusual chicharra activity on the farm. No one knew who uttered the name first, but it was in the world now as a whisper; it was those yellow eyes you think you see in the brush at night. Before you have a second look, they're gone. Whispers.

The workers sat by fires. "I'm telling you I saw her. Like La Lechuza, in the tree," a young boy said in a strained voice, higher pitched than usual.

A woman nursing a baby, patted its back softly. "I heard she wears a red bandana covering the bottom of her face like a bandita, big men's boots, and her blouse is stained black with dried blood from her wounded neck."

A man strummed on his guitar. "Yes, there she sits. Following you with her eyes and swinging her legs from the branches, judging your heart. Wasps nests in her hair and cicada shells cling to her skin. If you wear a hat, remove it out of respect. She deserves it." They all crossed themselves and nodded before the crackling heat of the fire.

The gringos put it down to heathen superstition; they were always looking for a way to get out of work. But it was all too much of a coincidence for the ones who knew better. The farm would soon be dead and those who earned their livelihood would have to move on. Billy's Uncle Ray stayed mostly in his large mansion taking inventory of all the things they could sell, but there was talk of him having to sell the farm itself to settle his mounting debts. His wife, too ashamed to be seen around town or at church, never left the house or took visitors anymore. Ray turned everyone away because as much as they offered thoughts and prayers for his loss, not a single thought or prayer would change the reality of the situation. "We appreciate your concern, but now is not a good time. Go on and pray for us." He closed the door, half the weight he was before, with his belt cinching his jeans tighter by the week. His round, rosy cheeks now hung as loose jowls covered in white and red stubble. If there were more money, he would have drunk whiskey from morning to night. He swallowed his pride with a glass of water that left a metallic taste in his mouth, before sitting down to write to his sister to expect them in California. They would only come with the clothes on their backs and start fresh.

*　　*　　*

On the day of Janice's funeral, Tanya stood next to Billy but felt alone. His hand held hers without any weight or affection. Black dresses and suits hung slack on bodies, tears and sweat patted with white handkerchiefs, hushed talk of how young she was, followed by a potluck at the church afterwards. Tanya was sick of this. Myrna's gloopy macaroni and cheese stuck to the roof of her mouth. She might have been eating spoonfuls of glue and paper. She forced herself to cry, thinking about the uncertainty of her young life whenever someone offered condolences. She couldn't care less about her dead friend. Perhaps all of this was a good thing, but not the way Billy imagined it. They could move on, maybe into a city and have a whole different existence. Tanya was weary of dusty farm life with strangers crawling around like silverfish. Dallas or Houston could be exciting. Billy could get a job with an oil company. They would be better off without the farm and the people who held them back. There were too many small-town girls willing to give it up to Billy and his beautiful blue eyes. She'd lost count how many times he had cheated on her, but marriage was forever. They said their vows before God, and she meant to keep those vows. Tanya would broach the subject with Billy on the drive home and maybe sweeten him up with a blow job on the side of the road. No one else knew him the way she did.

The road back home was empty. Dust danced in the headlights like ghosts looking for a body to inhabit. Soft country music played on the radio. Tanya was ready to make her big speech followed by roadside sex.

"Baby, I'm sick of funerals and I'm sick of Alice. Let's get out of here while we can."

Billy stared at the road, not knowing if he loved or hated the woman who sat next to him. It changed day to day. But what else was he supposed to do when she claimed she was pregnant three years ago? Turned out she lost it. He did the right thing even if it wasn't the thing he wanted. But what other woman would love him so much to turn a blind eye to his playing away? She knew who was boss.

"I'm close to having all that land to myself. I told you my plan already. Why would I want to give that all up to start over again as a grunt? No thank you. You'll make new friends. Why don't you have a baby? That'll keep you busy. I have to put my foot down on this one."

She opened her mouth to tell him she wasn't ready for a baby. Then it started as one insect on the windshield, followed by another. Billy turned on his windshield wipers to scare them away, but soon they were perching themselves on the wipers until the rubber blades could no longer move. The little bodies covered the headlights until the road went black.

"Fuck! What is this weird shit? I'm gonna have to get them off myself now."

As Billy yanked the steering wheel to the right, a bus slammed into the back of the truck. Both Tanya and Billy flew through the windshield in an explosion of glass and mangled metal. The bus screeched to a halt to radio in for help, but it was too late. Billy was pronounced dead on the scene as a headless corpse. However, Tanya clung to life. They rushed her to a local hospital, then transferred her to a larger hospital for specialized treatment in Houston. She managed to leave the farm after all.

*   *   *

Tanya opened her eyes for the first time since the accident in a hospital room that smelled of bleach, with bright light falling through the window. Her mother leaned over the bed in prayer, her mouth pencil thin and hair in a tight bun. In this sunlight she looked like a ghoulish scarecrow with her eyelashes, eyebrows and hair the same pale shade of straw. Her eyes scanned Tanya's body, her hands hovering above as if they had the power to resurrect it. "Thank Jesus you're awake."

Tanya readied her voice to speak but found she could not. She tried to move her arms, legs and neck without success. With only the ability to see and hear, she was trapped in her own body. Her mother must have sensed the worry in her eyes because, instead of praying, she averted her gaze to the other side of the room. Tanya wondered if she could still make facial expressions. The last thing she remembered was the cicadas flying out of the wreckage and into the air, their shadows from the lights of the bus making them appear as large as vultures. Tanya couldn't feel much of anything, but she could sense tears falling from the corners of her eyes.

"We're gonna pray for a miracle. The doctor says you broke your spinal column and things don't look exactly positive at this moment, but we put our faith in a higher medicine. The only medicine we need." Her mother's pity filled Tanya with vitriol. Stupid woman and all her faith in something that wasn't real.

Nobody was going to save her. A black fluttering spot disrupted the light coming through her window. It was a cicada. Tanya knew this would be the last time she would see her mother again, never to walk or talk. *She* was coming for her. Tanya knew she would be held in a prison of her own making before being consumed.

After her mother left for the day, the nurses came in to check the catheter and give her a sponge bath. Tanya was ready to die after a day of lying on her back with only the ability to control her eyes. Never again would she have the pleasure of tasting food, drinking beer, making love, laughing out loud. Her dreams had been snatched away from her in a moment, a moment she had no control over. This was not how she wanted to live. She was only twenty-two years old.

Cicadas had been gathered on the window since noon; it wouldn't be long now. Death would come and this purgatory would be over. Tanya believed there was nothing after you die or anything beyond the bounds of the earth, just nothing. It could all be flat for all she knew or cared.

She stared at the dark ceiling, waiting for the ghost of the murdered Mexican woman to claim her revenge. Instead it was just the song of the cicadas chanting, "La Reina de Las Chicharras", over and over. When she closed her eyes to sleep, all she could see was Milagros breaking loose from the tree. Insects of all variety poured from her eyes and mouth, crawling from beneath her clothing. Tanya could physically feel her throat tighten and her heart beat erratically as Milagros slowly moved closer, one steady foot in front of the other, expanding time. In Tanya's vision it was she tied to that tree. Their hate was mutual, but now Tanya writhed powerlessly beneath the ropes. Tanya imagined herself being feasted upon by each little creature that detached itself from Milagros. Skin cell by skin cell they would flay her to the bone. Milagros watched in boiling contempt through the one eye that remained open.

⋆　　⋆　　⋆

It was morning again. Tanya was stunned to be still alive in her sack of skin. She couldn't remember when she dozed off the night before as she waited to be set free. Her eyes darted to the window, which appeared clear, without a trace of the cicadas. The creak of the door and voice of the nurse made her jump inside.

"Good morning, Tanya. Looks like another beautiful day!"

The cheerful nurse strode to the window and fully opened the curtains to a blinding sun. Tanya groaned mentally. The hospital routine was the same as the previous day, except a doctor came to inform her Billy was dead. Lucky him. It was strange she felt nothing hearing this news. If anything, there was a relief there would be one less person to envy. She hated the thought of him with anyone else while she could do nothing about it. It was better this way.

When the nurse left her to fall asleep, she thought she could feel her lips moving. By some miracle her mouth parted a few centimeters. She was ready to scream until her voice uttered, "La Reina de Las Chicharras." It danced out of her throat like a mystical chant, as if she were a witch trying to conjure something evil. As she continued to mumble these words, the mirror on the wall opposite her bed caught her eye. There was a figure staring back at her with insects pouring from gaping holes that resembled eyes, a nose and mouth, just like in her visions.

Milagros laughed at her with a shriek that sounded like the cry of a coyote. Tanya imagined herself shrinking. It was at that moment she knew she would be left to live for as long as her heart continued to pump blood. Eventually, her mother stopped visiting, because not only did her daughter lose her body, but also her mind, babbling some Spanish nonsense. What a terrible, awful tragedy for someone so young with so much more life to live.

*   *   *

I gave Pastor Rich a nod and left him staring at the empty pulpit.
He was either praying or thinking about those days when the seats
were always filled.

Before we left, I wanted to see Milagros one more time.
I kissed my fingers and placed them on the top of the simple
headstone. This was more than just a macabre curiosity. I wanted
some sense of truth. As a lawyer, it had been my job to seek
justice. That, and I had so much to prove. Both Veronica and
I were determined to make good on the sacrifices our parents,
and their parents, had made. My mother graduated with her
bachelor's degree at twenty-eight after years of struggling to
pay for it. She barely earned enough to feed us afterwards. Her
father joined the Air Force to educate himself through the G.I.
Bill. His parents were farm workers.

I started off fresh and enthusiastic until it was clear what I
knew mattered less than how tight my skirt was. Any 'No' that
screamed in my mind was a breathless 'Yes' by the time it reached
my lips. I thought the word 'exotic' was best used to describe a
bird or a destination, not a human. When the business meeting
moved from the office to dinner to the strip club, I was the one
to stay out, giving the girls bigger tips than the guys. The only
thing that separated me from them was two college degrees (only
in some cases) and pumps instead of platforms. I had done worse
to survive, to get ahead. To fit in. Hustler to hustler, I had to give
them respect.

By the time I was laid off I knew in my bones there was no
such thing as justice in this world, not in the way I imagined it
should be. My cousin was still locked up, having been denied
parole countless times. His full sentence would only be up in a
year. He missed what seemed like a lifetime. Unlike things like
gravity and the sun, justice is a commodity, like oil or cotton or

tobacco. Just like the things Hector bought and sold that made him a lot of money before he left banking.

When my law firm began to represent a news agency that actively promoted the mistreatment of migrants at the border and the use of ICE, I spoke up. I said I wanted nothing to do with that client. Not a week later, I was told to leave. I took the coward's way with a large check in my pocket. I was one person. What could I do? Trying to fit in and succeed in my adult life made me feel stripped of my identity. Poverty stripped me of advantages as a child. School debt stripped me of options after graduation. Being malleable and having a good time stripped me of my anger. Not having a father stripped me of my self-esteem.

But something was changing in me. My inexplicable love for Milagros felt like love being sown in myself.

"Hector, I know I've already overstayed my welcome, but I think I want to go to Mexico. That address could still be good, or the tenants might know something. If I could just hang out until I can arrange my travel? I'll pay you, of course."

He wasn't looking at me or Milagros or the church. His thoughts were far off.

"You want company? You know, I haven't left this place since I bought it. It might be time."

I was hoping he would ask. Secretly I hoped he would travel with me; his companionship was the most real relationship I'd experienced in a very long time. Hector had no obligation with the B&B for over a week; he just needed to be back in time for a team of ghost hunters from the SyFy Channel to film the house. They were paying a top rate for a show that would be aired on Halloween. I made him promise I could stay for that. My best friend in Philadelphia agreed to overnight my passport for the trip. I called my son to check in and tell him I loved him. He responded with single-word answers and grunts, the sound of video games in the background. In my desperation to spark a conversation, I told him we could take a trip together when I returned. His response was a tepid, "If you want." All I could do was wait or pray for a miracle with him.

It had been ages since I last visited Mexico. The first time was when I was nine years old. We drove all the way from San Antonio, Texas to Guadalajara, Mexico. I had never seen an outhouse before and I remember crying when my enchiladas were covered in some type of fresh white cheese that wasn't a bright orange goo that stretched like a never-ending elastic band. I was used to that in Texas. The candy was made from tamarind and the fruit covered in chamoy. There were no Nerds or Hubba Bubba. I wanted orange cheese and McDonald's. But I loved the Coke. The Coke in Mexico is made with sugar cane that gives it a sweetness that is an opiate for the mouth. The other time I traveled to Mexico was with a boyfriend in college. The culture we experienced was mainly between the sheets or in a tequila bottle. Now, I was returning as a non-Spanish speaker trying to do something meaningful for a woman who deserved to have her name known to all. Hector's flawless Spanish would be helpful in navigating our journey to San Luis Potosi, Mexico.

CHAPTER SIX

The address listed next to Milagros Santos' name was a whitewashed stucco building surrounded by a rusty iron fence. The yard was a beautiful mixture of large agave plants, hibiscus bushes and crawling bougainvilleas. A woman in her sixties or seventies with hair braided and clipped to her head in a bun stood in the front yard, feeding a dog that looked happier than the woman to see us. We might have shared the same ancestry as her; however, we still looked like tourists or intruders not from the neighborhood. Hector had to do the speaking.

Without so much as a breath, the old woman shouted into the open screened door, "Benny!" The scowl remained on her face despite Hector's ability to communicate fluently.

A man dressed in fitted jeans, t-shirt and Timberland boots exited the house. Both arms were covered in tattoos. He looked close to Hector's age. "How can I help you?" Hector and I were surprised he spoke to us in English.

"We're looking for the family of a woman. Her name was Milagros Santos. She left Mexico to work on a farm in the fifties. She never returned and whatever letters or money she sent might have stopped abruptly."

The man shook his head then looked at the old woman, who stopped feeding the dog. There was no mistaking the woman understood what was said. She wiped her face with her cotton apron, then shuffled inside without giving us a second look.

Benny looked back, torn between rushing inside and finding out what we had to say.

"Milagros is dead? Why don't we go up the street to a restaurant? My mother doesn't like strangers in the house."

We walked a few blocks in a residential area to a bustling street of daily life activity until we faced a restaurant with an open kitchen in the back. I paused to watch the women making fresh tortillas. The smell felt comforting and delicious, like my grandmother's house. I wanted to camp out in that kitchen to just sit and watch them methodically roll out dough on their stone slabs. Every movement was like an ancient ritual passed down generation to generation, a ballet of nourishment. The same can be said for making the perfect molé. Accordion-heavy music played from the main kitchen, with loud voices laughing and speaking. This restaurant had all the best things I remembered from my childhood.

Benny ordered Tecate beer and menudo for all of us. The pungent broth awoke my senses. The different chilis rolled in my mouth, pricking the inside of my cheeks and the back of my throat. It delighted me in ways I'd forgotten existed. Hominy and tripe bobbed in the delicious liquid. My mouth felt alive. My body felt satiated the more I ate, like it had not been fed in years, and in some ways it had not. I was always the first to try any new diet that claimed to brighten my skin or shed quick pounds. I tried my hardest to drink my carbs and sugar instead of chewing them. My body didn't want to be punished any longer. It needed to feed.

"Milagros would have been my great aunt. I think. You know how it is in our families. Everyone is an aunt of a sister of a cousin once removed. I heard stories about her leaving to the States, but we never knew anything after her letters stopped. I went to the farm years ago when I was studying. It was in the hands of the bank and no one knew anything there either. As a young kid more interested in having a good time, I just left it and returned to my life. What do you know?"

I was slurping the menudo when I noticed both men staring at me.

"Oh, sorry. Well, it's a long story, but your aunt was a victim of a hate crime. Though in some ways she still exists as a story." Hector and I recounted every last detail to Benny. His foot tapped the floor nervously while he took long drinks from his beer, leaving the menudo untouched. I helped myself to the side of his corn tortillas once mine were finished to scrape my bowl clean. I'd never tasted anything as wonderful as a simple paste of corn that is flattened and grilled.

"You should know Milagros was a twin. My great aunt was her twin."

Hector and I looked at each other. I wiped away the wetness on my lips left from my greedy eating. I felt something big in this entire puzzle might be revealed. "And where is your aunt?"

Before Benny said anything, he called over the waitress to order three shots of Mezcal. "This is on me before we go to see her."

I felt confused, not that I wasn't going to drink this, but the sense of mystery deepened. "Why do we need this before seeing her?"

Benny took the shot of smooth liquid smoke, puckering his lips after. "When I'm there I feel there is a presence, a shadow. I can't decide if it is good or bad, but I know I am not alone, and it scares me. As a doctor, to feel things I can't study or explain makes me uncomfortable. When I was just a boy, I was fascinated by my aunt, how she could be awake and asleep at the same time. On one occasion when I was maybe eight or nine, my family prayed in Concepcion's bedroom in the house where you found us. I played on my own in the living room, too young to join the prayer. I turned towards the bathroom because I was sure someone had walked out and watched me as I played. It was seconds, but the silhouette of a woman appeared then disappeared. I screamed and screamed, breaking up the prayer circle. Boy, did I get it for causing a fuss over nothing. Since then, whenever I'm around Concepcion, I sense whatever appeared in the doorway of the bathroom."

"I come from a family of curanderos," Hector said, "and I've spent my adult life with numbers because I don't like the supernatural. I know the feeling." He gulped his shot first, squeezing his eyes as he swallowed.

I had to ask. "What did she look like?"

Benny peered into his beer bottle for remnants before answering. "A woman without any skin."

After that, I needed my shot. My dream. There had to be an explanation, something we all had heard or seen. I needed another shot after that first one but felt self-conscious ordering another to stop the internal hemorrhaging of confusion and fear, falling deeper into a black spot without any control over what happens next.

"Hey, Belinda. Didn't you tell me about a dream like that? A woman?"

I nodded and looked at Benny. Hector's head turned from my face to Benny's. None of us wanted to say out loud that something strange had brought us together. Benny raised his hand to call the waitress over for another shot.

Afterwards, I paid since I'd practically finished both Benny and Hector's meals while they talked about their experiences in America. I expected to return to the house where we found Benny, but instead we walked for twenty minutes through a middle-class neighborhood before entering a smart apartment building with a doorman, who greeted Benny then looked at us with suspicion.

"My aunt is in a state doctors can't explain. She is basically catatonic. She suffered a stroke in 1952 at the age of twenty. It was completely out of the blue. Even today doctors can't explain what happened. Every test I have had done on her shows no brain trauma from a stroke or seizure."

I didn't want the elevator to stop. I didn't want to see his great aunt, and the menudo was a twisted ball of pigs feet and chili in my stomach.

The apartment was small, with one bedroom, but clean, full of natural light from large windows that extended the length of the wall. A nurse stood in a galley kitchen preparing coffee. Strangely, I didn't feel any presence or bad vibes. It was quiet and calm, like entering an empty church. In the bedroom, Concepcion lay in one of those adjustable beds, which was in an upright position surrounded by flowers and glass column candles of various saints. Watery, wide eyes stared out the single window that faced her bed. Her hair was tightly braided, and she wore a long, pale yellow nightgown. Her fingers were manicured. Over one eye, extending from the top of her eyebrow to the bottom of her nose, was a raised strawberry birthmark. Unlike those of people with fair skin, the birthmark was a deep shade of red, almost purple. It reminded me of an exploding star. A sepia photo of two identical women sat next to her bed in a gold frame. The women were beautiful, with dark brown skin and lustrous black hair resting on their shoulders. Their hands were intertwined as they stared directly into the camera. The four eyes were so large and black they were almost frightening in their stoic gaze. It was like four eclipses happening at once.

I garnered the courage to sit next to the woman in a chair I suspected Benny and the nurse had spent hours in. Before I could get any words out, a small sound escaped her grooved lips. At first I thought I imagined it, but I knew it was real when Benny rushed to her bedside.

Her eyes shifted towards me. "Lo se." I knew enough high-school Spanish to understand she was saying, "I know."

What did she know? That her twin was dead, and I knew what happened to her? Did she know I was trying to do something decent, for once? I just blurted it all out.

"Milagros is no longer here. She was murdered and I want to bring her body back to you, her family, and erect a marker at the tree where she died. I'm very sorry for your loss."

The old woman's eyes grew larger as tears fell from the corners. She repeated, "Lo se."

There was something dark beneath the saggy eyelids that I couldn't read. She was a helpless old woman unable to move, but in that moment, I feared she might jump from the bed and rip out my throat.

Benny was weeping. I couldn't read if he was happy or confused. "Can you please leave us alone for a moment? I'd like to do a check on her." Hector and I left the room, closing the door behind us.

The nurse sat at a small table against the window, staring in her coffee cup. I thought she would have shown more emotion after her only patient spoke for the first time since 1952. Instead she motioned for us to come over.

"I will speak English since you are not local and that is what you are speaking to Benny. Mexicans from America, I take it. Anyway, that woman is not what she seems. I heard you talk about her twin, Milagros. This is a small town, you know. The families have been here for years. I was told about those twins. Sweet, but strange. Her people are originally from Chiapas, if you couldn't tell by how dark she is. I think one of the men was a Zapatista. So that means trouble already. And that birthmark. Dios. They never ever went to church, kept to themselves. People whispered they were witches. The neighborhood strays would whimper away when they approached. Milagros left after a boy kept hounding her for a date. Now, this wasn't just any boy. His father was the chief of police. She and her sister were waiting for the bus one day when the boy came looking for trouble. He got rough with her, trying to steal a kiss and grab her body. People looked on but did nothing. When the bus arrived, he let go of her. People at the bus stop remembered seeing the twins' faces side by side in the back of the bus window with their lips moving, eyes unblinking. Not a few minutes later that boy was struck by a different bus. The investigation went on and on. That is why the town started whispering about them. After the accident they were ill for days. Then miraculously they were better than ever. There was too much talk after that, so she left. They had a family friend working in the States through the Bracero program who would come back and forth between jobs. When he was heading back north, they paid him to take Milagros along into Texas, where he said he knew she would have an easier time than in other farming states. Her family hoped to leave too with the money Milagros would send back. Concepcion stayed to help their parents." She paused and craned her neck past us to be sure the door was not opening.

"My mother told me that the family was forced to seek an exorcism after the stroke because there was nothing wrong with Concepcion. They thought it could be black magic or something evil at work. When the priest arrived at their home he immediately left after he found out not only was she not an active Catholic, but she wasn't even a Christian. In her bedroom, on an altar she made with her sister, they found a depiction of Santa Muerte. The priest did not like that. They begged him to come back, saying they did believe in God, but also practiced the old ways. That was not a sin if their intent was good. The priest also said he felt like they were not alone in her room. Something breathed down his neck during his entire visit. He never wanted to go back."

"What do you believe? Have you ever felt like you were not alone here?" I asked.

She sipped her coffee, drilling holes into my eyes with her own. "I have my faith and it protects me. So, no. I have never

felt anything here. Let me ask you, are you only here to bring
Milagros rest?"

Hector tapped his finger against the table. "I own the farm
where she was murdered. Milagros has become something of an
urban legend. La Reina de Las Chicharras."

"Is that so? Haven't heard of it. Well, then, I believe those
twins brought something into this world that doesn't belong. You
mentioned Milagros was murdered? Who knows what she might
have done with her dying breath? Maybe she made a pact with
the Devil."

Before she could speak again, the door opened. Benny's eyes
were red. He held a rosary in his hand and a stethoscope around
his neck. "You know she is the reason I became a doctor."

Hector placed an arm on Benny's shoulder and Benny returned
the gesture. I stood, feeling awkward in a moment they seemed to
share. Concepcion didn't speak again. Instead she fell asleep with
her hands at her side, looking at peace, with her body covered
with a light blanket. Benny didn't want to disturb her with the
apartment being so small, so we left. I parted ways with Hector and
Benny, feeling like the third wheel as they were fast friends talking
in and out of Spanish. Benny, short for Benigno, was a doctor in
San Luis Potosi. He discounted any gossip about his family as just
that: gossip. Their family luck changed years after Concepcion fell
into her catatonic state. A well-respected, wealthy doctor paid the
family to study her periodically. Benny was always curious when
Dr. Rey was around, and the old doctor didn't mind entertaining
the young boy's questions. When Dr. Rey retired, he promised
to pay for Benny's education if he maintained his grades. Benny
not only maintained his grades, but excelled.

I returned to my single motel room to sleep or masturbate
or whatever else I could do to help me focus and think about
the things that had transpired. What exactly did I want out of
this trip, which was taking a turn for the strange? Was Milagros

haunting the farm and her family? The motel was simple with basic furniture and a small TV with bad reception. The loud mini fridge was fully stocked with *Topo Chico* water. I could drink that water like wine. I fell asleep earlier than I ever would normally. Who was the woman without any skin?

CHAPTER SEVEN

Mictecacíhuatl, Queen of the Dead, speaks from Mictlan

May I tell you my side of the story? Sometimes the dead deserve to be amongst the living and some of the living should long be dead or never born at all. But that is not the way of life. Just ask the women who have died in childbirth. They are my handmaidens down here, in Mictlan, the place you call the underworld. I reside here, to preside over the bones of the dead with my king, who has been enjoying his retirement from worship. He never recovered from the deep sorrow that invaded his soul after the slaughter by the conquistadors.. He is a pussycat, really, even though he is more of a dog person. I am the one they should have feared.

On this particular day, I walked on a road near my home. A single drop of blood dripped on my robe. With one finger I brought it to my mouth, taking in its essence. Its sweetness was familiar to me. When I looked above, there was nothing there, and I continued on. Later, as I sat reading, a small cry alerted me to a crime I could not ignore. And so many heinous acts of evil I have watched since the inception of time. I traveled through the eye of a little spider to a ceiba tree where I found the voice that filled me with such despair. It was a young woman about to perish by the hands of other cruel, hate-filled humans. There was no need for me to look into their hearts to see their wickedness. To say I was displeased is an understatement. I was furious, and in my fury, I poured my power into the earth and the tree and the beautiful creatures of the land to take vengeance on behalf of this innocent. Their venom would be more toxic and their will my own, because this innocent was special. She had the blood of magic. Her ancestor, Ikal, was a great priest who worshipped me with such fervor, all his sacrifices were pleasing to me. In fact, he died protecting my divine countenance chiseled in stone as it dripped in the precious blood of those who sailed upon the wind of greed and domination. For a time, they cowered before the ferocity of our warriors dressed in vividly painted armor as jaguars. They knew we sacrificed our captives. Milagros's noble priest ancestor refused to be a slave and, in a final act of defiance, he was cut down. That is why I heard her call. The currency of loyalty and blood surpasses anything that can be exchanged by hand.

I clipped a string of my heart muscle and gave it to another spider to wrap in a parcel of webbing for the chicharra to feed upon. My essence, once inside the little insect, perched upon the dying woman's collar bone. I asked her what she wished of me. In a voice that was silent to everyone but me, she said she wanted blood-for-blood vengeance. She wanted to live on. I should visit her twin and tell her of all that had happened. Together they were special. Her heart wanted to make love to the Devil so she may sell her soul for life, or revenge. In that moment I wanted to kiss her forehead and stroke her head, like a mother would console a small child after a bad dream. I explained I could not bring her back to life as she was dying. That is final. The particles of her soul were already beginning to disperse and make their way to my kingdom. I allowed half of her soul to remain on her world while the other stayed with me, for a cost. Blood. Worship. Life. I informed her there was no such thing as the Devil. The closest she would ever come to such a monster stood in front of her. If she wanted to peer into the skull of the grotesque, she should open her eyes and see her tormentors. One of them tried to flee. I say tried because that little fish would not escape my hook. She saw my image and it was my intention for all to see me once more in my horrible beauty painted in wrath.

Feeding this power of justice over the ages of time would require a sacrifice by everyone. Punishment has a dear price. Both she and her twin would have to give of themselves in blood and spirit. And I wanted punishment too. The invaders must have thought themselves gods because they forced their seed on the women of the brown soil to create a different race of offspring. It is because of those invaders long ago that I am no longer worshipped. All that blood spilled in the name of another god forced me to return to my universe outside of this one. But let it be known once and for all, the known space beyond is like a string of polished jade stones, tightly coiled so that each one gently touches another. Each stone is a different universe with unique beings, gods and laws. When these stones touch there is nothing to stop an exchange of energy. When universes collide is when you see and feel those things that you fear.

The legend of the humans says my visage is flayed, and this is indeed true. All you see when you gaze upon me is striated ropes of muscle as taut as the strings of a warrior's bow. My veins are prominent with their shades of blue and dark red. Mostly they beat steadily except when in the throes of sex with my love. But in our universe, no one is tethered by such a delicate thing as skin. Being skinless has given us a freedom that humans do not enjoy. During sex our bodies intertwine, making the experience so much more intense. There is nowhere to hide or fake as every muscle spasm can be seen and felt. Slick with blood, we move in and out of each other until our bodies resemble a sheet of flesh that is truly two beings becoming one. It is quite a sad thing to see so much misery caused by skin. As much as I hated to leave this bauble of paradise, once those boats set foot upon our chosen home, I knew it would only be a matter of time before we would be forced to flee. The god of the boat people is a jealous god.

It is also true the home I share with my husband is a windowless box. The walls and columns that keep my residence standing are made from the tightly compacted bones of the dead. The hallways are made from skulls that look out from the walls, whispering to me their deeds in life or their song of praise for allowing their presence in my home. There is one single room without anyone at all. Looking after souls is a deafening job. Even we need a place to retreat to for solace and quiet. If I had not been at rest in my darkened windowless room, I might not have heard the cry of Milagros until it was too late, and her cry made me ache. It made me think of all the screams of my devotees as they were murdered by demons on horseback. Powerlessness is a horrible thing to feel. Constant fear is a rope, a sword, a whip cutting into flesh and consciousness until you become a walking dead thing.

I called upon the cicada perched upon her neck to collect half of her soul for safekeeping until the time came for her to change form for good. The cicada shell with her soul would rest in my womb. When she feels her vengeance is full and my belly has grown large, I will bring her back. She will be my daughter in this otherworld. For now, she will be La Reina de Las Chicharras. I would be lying if I said it didn't feel good, to be halfway into the world of the living again. The tales of our existence have been denounced. We are things of fiction, dusty artifacts preserved behind glass, mere characters created by early civilizations to explain their world. Science says we do not exist.. But next time you hear that scratch or howl or have a sensation of unease, it is not science in the room; it could be one of us, passing through your realm. The otherworld is closer than you think because eyes are like skin, soft barriers that prevent enlightenment instead of bringing you closer to the truth.

CHAPTER EIGHT

When I could just feel the sunlight on my eyelids, I received a call from Hector.

"Something is wrong. Very, very wrong. Benny asked me to call you. The nurse left a message he couldn't understand and now she isn't answering her phone." His voice and what he said almost didn't register as I struggled to wake up. It was only the fear in his tone that roused me enough to brush my teeth and pull back my hair. Coffee would have to wait. The nurse had strict instructions to keep her phone on at all times after Concepcion decided to speak. She lived there Monday to Friday, sleeping on the pull-out bed in the front room, her only job being to care for Concepcion, who needed constant medical attention. In all her years of employment, there had never been an emergency or anything out of the ordinary.

Hector and Benny met me at the motel, which was halfway between the apartment building and Benny's home. We walked rapidly towards the apartment building in silence. It felt wrong to ask how their night went with Benny being in such a distressed state. This entire journey and the story of Milagros was becoming something none of us expected. It was a muddled tale taking a life of its own within our lives. You hear about weird shit; rarely do you experience it. Benny's first thought was his aunt might be alone due to some emergency the nurse might be experiencing, or they were robbed. The latter was unlikely because it was a safe neighborhood and when Benny called the doorman, he said no one he didn't know had been in or out. The doorman was waiting for us when we arrived at the apartment.

"Señor, I can't open the door. The key you gave me for an emergency isn't working either. I've tried everything! I'm sorry I couldn't be more help." The old man continued to pull on his moustache, his distress as great as Benny's because he had worked there nearly as long as Concepcion was a tenant.

"It's okay. We'll all go up. Maybe it's nothing." Benny fidgeted in silence during the extended ride to the fifth floor. The tension smothered our words and all we could do was stare at the doors until they opened.

When we got off the elevator, the door to Concepcion's apartment opened as we approached. We could not see who was there. Benny sprinted ahead with us following. The immediate scent of blood filled our nostrils like a muggy blanket of heat on skin, the kind you feel when you exit a plane somewhere humid. The nurse lay on the floor with her neck sliced open, the esophagus hanging out of the gash like a tongue. Concepcion kneeled over the body, covered in blood, with her nightgown looking like a second red skin. We didn't know if it all belonged to the nurse or if Concepcion herself was somehow injured. There was so much of it. The doorman stumbled out of the room and ran.

Without a single strand of hair out of place, Concepcion whispered, "La Reina de Las Chicharras." She turned to face us and spoke in Spanish. I turned to Benny and Hector, who both looked to be in shock.

"Wha-what is she saying?" Hector stammered,

"Uhhh. She says Milagros needs to be fed. She will be back soon." Concepcion looked at me, pointing the blade towards my abdomen. Her eyes were soft and pleading and she spoke again in a language I hated myself for not speaking. It made me feel lost. Between worlds.

With tears in his eyes Benny spoke and took a step forward. "She says, 'Belinda, you are so empty. Let her fill you up. Let her love shine through you. No one will harm you and you will never feel lonely again. The Queen is real!'"

I shook my head, wanting to burst into sobs and run away, like I always did.

Both men, who were twice my size, looked as if they might run, too. Benny gawked in shock with his eyes fixed on the opening in the nurse's neck leaking blood in a steady flow. As a doctor I would have expected him to rush into action. I don't think this scene of murder registered with his brain; this was a woman he had only known in one way. I viewed this differently as an outsider, the horror not consuming me as it did him. Truth be told, Concepcion's words comforted me. I wanted to hear them, feel them. I kept my eyes on the old woman and not the dead body.

"Concepcion." She looked wild when I acknowledged her. Something vibrated from her body that called me forward. I knew she didn't mean to harm any of us. I pointed to the knife and extended my hand, trying to smile. She grinned back at me, then looked at Benny, tears falling from her eyes.

Her voice cracked. She appeared to have something heartfelt to say to Benny.

"How did you..." Benny managed to say between sobs. Hector and Benny exchanged glances.

I was nearing Concepcion one step at a time. There was no way this frail lady would be a match for me. I had to continue to look at her face; otherwise I might have vomited with the sight of the body at our feet. My plan was to grab her waist with one hand and her wrist holding the knife with the other. I hoped one of the guys would take the opportunity to snatch the weapon away.

She spoke again, too calm for someone who'd just committed a murder, her eyes flat and dark as if she were tunneling to somewhere far from here.

The old woman brought the blade to her neck and sliced clean through with a swift, firm grip. Warm spray hit my eyes and mouth. Hector and Benny screamed. I could only watch the blood exit her body as she collapsed to the floor. The existing pool of blood increased in size as it surrounded me. It looked as if I was stepping into a lake of crimson, a place of baptism. It was so dark there was no telling how deep it could be. Was it even blood? It could have been a mirror.

Another scream, this one female, brought me back to the crime scene. A neighbor at the open doorway stared at the two dead bodies. She only looked away to scramble around her purse to find her phone. Back to his senses, Benny kneeled in the puddle of blood, clutching the lifeless body of Concepcion. Tears and snot covered his face in a wet mask, with the rest of him slathered in her blood. Neither Hector nor I could move. Where would we go? What could we do? I could tell Hector wanted to run to Benny, scoop him up in his arms. He held back.

I went to Hector's side. "What did she say? What happened?"

He shook his head and wiped his tears. "She told Benny to have a good life and find love because this world is tired. She said I looked like a nice boy. How…how did she know? Before she…"

His voice cracked and lips quivered.

"Hector, you don't have to say any more."

"No. It sounded important. She said her magic is gone. 'It is for the new life. I will feed her now.'"

I wrapped my arms around Hector as we both cried together at this tragedy.

In a matter of minutes, the police and an ambulance arrived with a crowd of people rushing through the door. The doorman had called the police when he made it back to his desk. They also received the call from the woman, who was being interrogated in the corridor. There was nothing we could do except answer their questions, which we had no answers to. Benny wasn't angry and he didn't blame us for showing up and bringing all this doom into his life, but he also didn't want us around much longer. Hector offered to stay and help, but Benny was adamant his family would not want outsiders interfering in their business. These past few days were beyond anything he could have imagined happening with Concepcion. Everyone assumed one day she would be found peacefully gone in her bed. Everything he'd learned in medicine was challenged by the macabre twist of events. Benny wanted time to investigate on his own. He thanked us for telling him about Milagros; however, her body could stay where it was. A plaque on the tree where she perished was enough. After all the affairs were taken care of here, he would come pay his respects. The doctors thought Concepcion might have been in some state of psychosis after awakening. In her disturbed state of mind, she killed the nurse. It was all just a terrible accident that no one could have predicted. Some things even science or medicine could not explain.

★   ★   ★

Benny opened the door to Concepcion's apartment, wishing someone else could do this. His mind and body felt continually bogged down in a blanket of exhaustion, even after going to bed every night before nine p.m. and sleeping every day until noon. Maybe he shouldn't have told Hector and Belinda to leave. No, it was better this way. He took a single step inside. A black stain still covered the spot on the floor where the nurse and Concepcion had bled out. It reminded him of an ugly bruise or a blood clot. The urge to leave overwhelmed him, but this was the third time he put this off. All of that after looking for someone he could pay to do this job for him. But he wanted one more look to try to understand it all. Maybe his memory would shed light on her condition, which had made no sense.

He shut the door behind him and went straight to the bedroom to clear out the room and gather Concepcion's few belongings. It smelled like her. The room felt off without her looking out the window. Benny approached the unmade bed and touched the soft sheets that would be thrown away instead of reused. The horror of what had happened here had to be forgotten, at least for a little while. Otherwise the grief would overtake him. He fell to his knees, leaning his arms and forehead against the mattress. The sobs rolled out of him quietly until controlling them became too much. As he continued to weep, he squeezed the edges of the mattress until his hands were balled into fists.

Something solid pressed against his forehead. He pulled back and wiped his eyes. With his right hand, he touched the hard spot. Benny lifted the fitted sheet. On the side of the mattress, a small slit with shredded threads caught his eye. He wiggled his hand into the opening. It was a tight fit, but he managed to feel a sharp corner. Benny jumped to his feet and dashed into the kitchen to grab a knife. He paused as he noticed a blade was missing from the block. It took him back to the trauma. He shook his head and grabbed another, then took big strides back to the bedroom.

With his free hand, he pulled the sheet completely off the bed and felt around the top of the mattress until he found the outline of the hidden thing. One hand ran against the edge while the knife sawed around the object, which was in the shape of a book. He peeled off the flap of the mattress. He saw a small notebook with a pen tucked into the metal spiral spine. The nurse had complained she misplaced it a few months back. Benny stared at the notebook with fear and confusion. What the hell was happening? There was no way, no fucking way Concepcion put it in there. Why would the nurse turn the apartment upside down for something she deliberately hid? He could feel himself shaking. It seemed like the presence he always felt was standing right behind him. Benny whipped his head around to be sure. It was only the darkness of the open bathroom and the outline of the showerhead. He turned back to the bed and reached for the notebook. There was only one way to find out.

He sat on the floor next to the torn mattress with the notebook in hand. The first few pages were nothing but lists of errands and groceries written by the nurse. Halfway through, he noticed a different penmanship on one page. *Concepcion y Milagros* was scrawled at the top.

★   ★   ★

Arturo watched Milagros. The way she carried herself with a quiet confidence intrigued him. He longed to pull the single braid that fell just above her waist. From the back of the church he had spied her on previous occasions on her knees next to another young woman, Mariposa. Milagros and Mariposa were school friends turned something else he didn't care to mention. He knew Mariposa's family because both of their fathers worked on the police force, except his was the chief. The two women exchanged touches so stealthily you had to really be looking to notice. It aroused him, thinking of them, but he only wanted Milagros, and he would have her. What else would a girl like her do with her life? She wasn't special. Throughout school she was meek and simple. Not too smart, but not a dimwit either. Easy to mold, he thought. No one likes a difficult, loud, or loose female.

"Find a sweet girl to make your wife, like your mother," his father had told him. "She has all my uniforms ready and can cook all my favorite meals. You will be busy, my son, when you start your job with me."

★   ★   ★

Milagros and her sister chose fruit and vegetables at the market stall. It was busy, but once they were beyond the thick of the crowd, Arturo caught up to them.

"Milagros, you still haven't responded to my invitation for an evening out."

Milagros and Concepcion continued to walk towards their home not far from the town center. "Go away, Arturo. She told you many times she is not interested."

"Shut up. You're just jealous because no one will want you with that thing on your face."

Milagros swung her head in his direction. "Don't talk to my sister like that. And she has plenty of men who want her, not that it matters, or is any of your business. I'm warning you, leave me alone."

Arturo stood close enough to her so that only she could hear what he whispered. The breath escaping his nose puffed against her earlobe. He held on to her by the elbow, his thumb rubbing the joint on the inside of her arm. His cologne and sweat was a sickly mixture she wanted to run from.

"I'm warning *you*. You don't think I've seen you with Mariposa? Those stolen touches. You will be mine, and if you won't, I'll let everyone know about your little crush. You know as well as I do it can never be. Besides, you'll forget about her on our wedding night. The things you'll have to let me do to you."

Milagros felt sick to her stomach. Her revulsion and sorrow were worse than a festering wound. He took the liberty of brushing the back of his hand against her breast then biting his lip. In that moment Milagros knew if she did not end him, this game of cat and mouse would never end either. If Milagros had a sheathed knife at her waist, it would be stuck into his balls until it reached the top of his throat. Like a butchered pig. But there was no knife. She yanked her arm away and grabbed her sister's hand before storming off.

"I will see you around, my love!" Arturo shouted behind them.

*　　*　　*

It was a relief to be in the safety and comfort of their modest two-bedroom home. Milagros paced in the living room. It was usually cool, but the heat of the day was suffocating her. "I need to be free of him. How dare he use my love against me!"

Milagros looked to Concepcion, knowing she understood the thorn of forbidden love. She regularly shared the bed of a married man, a vaquero, when he visited the town. Concepcion told her that the passion between them felt good when he was around because long weeks of travel left him sex-starved and hungry. He gave her everything she needed from a man, without burdening her with the duties of a wife. They talked for hours in bed about life, what they wanted in their later years.

His satchel was always filled with herbs and plants from various parts of Mexico that Concepcion used for her rituals. Sometimes he brought plundered treasure from their ancestors. Blades, stone idols, things that were important for her to preserve for a reason she did not know. All of these sat in a small dresser in her room. On top of the dresser was where she and Milagros left offerings to their ancestors who had passed, fresh flowers from their garden, a smooth disk of obsidian, along with prayer cards printed with Catholic saints. A small, rare image of Santa Muerte.

"What do you want to do, Milagros?"

Milagros looked at her with weary eyes. "We should put the oranges on the altar. I want to pray, really pray."

They sat at the edge of Concepcion's bed looking at their reflection in the mirror in the center of the altar. Milagros breathed in and out slowly. *Focus.* She saw her intention in her mind's eye. In the mirror she could see her long braid rise up by itself and slowly coil around her neck. A specter of Arturo's face appeared behind her. Then his fingers gripped the noose of hair. Milagros knew what she had to do. But when?

★   ★   ★

"That was the worst film I have ever seen!" laughed Concepcion. The sisters walked together to the bus stop after an afternoon of helping their father at the secondhand shop and taking in a movie with the money he gave them as wages. "You should save your money!" their mother would scold, but there was time for that. They wanted to have fun, enjoy life.

In a matter of seconds, the mood turned dark like a solar eclipse. "Move behind everyone. It's Arturo," Milagros whispered. It was too late. He spotted them. She wondered how he was always around.

"So, have you made a decision? In front of all these people who also know my father. Say yes to be my wife." He seemed drunk, with bloodshot eyes, his feet trying to catch themselves. Milagros weaved through the crowd around a bus stop.

"Stop moving away from me. Who do you think you are? I'm trying to give you a better life. You need to appreciate what a man can offer you. My mother says I shouldn't waste my time on you in case our baby comes out looking like your sister."

Both women stopped. Concepcion took a step towards Arturo, but Milagros put an arm in front of her waist. "In front of all these people and whatever else is listening in the heavens, I will never be yours and my body is my own. Don't touch me. Say what you want. But I warned you, Arturo." The crowd watched the scene in silence. No one stopped Arturo's harassment.

"Then give me a kiss." He pulled her hard by the waist with one hand while yanking her braid with the other.

"I feed you to the dogs!" Milagros screamed with all the oxygen in her lungs and will in her heart. One woman crossed herself, seeing the rage on Milagros's face. It was the mask of the Devil in the body of a young girl who shook and growled. Concepcion and Milagros fled into the bus that waited and scurried to the back window. They didn't even know the destination of the vehicle. Through the black exhaust they could see Arturo. With hands clasped, small crescents of blood appeared as their nails dug so tightly into each other's flesh.

"Are you ready to do this, Concepcion?"

"Yes. Let him answer for his evil and may his body go to the beasts. I was going to just scare him off. Now he will be gone forever."

Never in their lives could they explain how they made things happen when they were together. Their will tunneled to a singularity where they saw what they wanted. It played in their mind and they said it without sound with their lips.

A small stray dog with protruding ribs and mangy hair approached Arturo. It licked his hand. "Get out of here, you mutt!" He kicked the dog, which yelped with this sudden violence. The dog proceeded to cross the road with Arturo behind. But Arturo didn't see the speeding truck swerve around the dog until it was too late to jump out of its way.

Arturo lay in a heap of torn guts and flesh, his skull a crushed mass of brain tissue and blood. A slight breeze blew his hair like the fur of roadkill getting continually run over.

The stray ran to the mess. It sniffed a few times, then took hungry mouthfuls of his body. The fur around its mouth dripped with blood as it relished this unexpected meal.

A crowd at the bus stop and other bystanders watched on in horror. Three women looked at Milagros and Concepcion in the back of the bus, their cold stare filled with intent. One of the women crossed herself before elbowing a stranger.

"Look at them. Isn't that the girl he was bothering? Did you hear what she said? This was no accident."

The incident changed everything. A small town loves and hates its secrets. Concepcion and Milagros walked with whispers in their wake. Gossip and suspicious eyes trailed like a mud-sodden cloak behind them. Their mother worked at the local clinic, but people didn't want her near their children. The secondhand store her father ran was dead.

★   ★   ★

"I'll leave. It's the only way. Business will get better, and if you want to still relocate, fine. Let me do this. Papa says his friend is heading to Texas for work with the Bracero program. He can sneak me in."

Concepcion threw her bra on a chair as she changed for bed. "I hate this. Why are we being punished? If only they knew. But no one would believe us. Arturo had all the power and he knew that. I had to take that power from him."

Milagros stood from her bed and pulled out a letter from the top drawer.

"Just do one thing for me. Please give a letter to Mariposa."

Concepcion shook her head. "I'll try but we're being shunned. Maybe I can sneak around the church. God knows I can't get close to her."

"Whatever you can do. Thank you, sister."

Milagros left at sunset with as much home cooking she could carry without it spoiling.

"You don't have to do this," her parents pleaded, but Milagros had made up her mind. They cried into each other's shoulders before their family friend, Gustavo, told them it was time to hit the road. The clouds stretched across the sky, forming what looked like the head of a serpent. Stray white wisps that could have been feathers jutted out in all directions. The sun bled hues of red and pink from the center of the mouth.. She wondered if the Texas sky would be as expansive and beautiful. Soon she would have a new life in a new country she had never intended on visiting. What would await her in that strange land? The entire drive she refused to speak. Her soul felt like a lost letter, tumbling in the wind without a sender or anyone to receive it.

★   ★   ★

After Milagros left, Concepcion didn't feel the same. Even the times she shared with her lover felt less warm. Then one night as she lay in bed, her throat seized, and her heart collapsed in on itself before each small cell floated away like fruit flies. Her vision tunneled to the bottom of a cenote, where a small door waited for her. Oxygen bubbles rose past her face. The rest of the water was too dark to see. She reached out to push the door open. More darkness, until an arm without skin reached out and pulled her through. Concepcion lay in bed with her eyes unmoving, but knowing Milagros was gone.

"Open your eyes, Concepcion, and breathe."

On her hands and knees, Concepcion clutched her throat, thinking she was still underwater. The floor was wet and slippery. The light was dim and warped shadows snaked across her hand. She slowly looked up to the voice. The sight nearly made Concepcion tumble back. A petite nude figure of muscle, viscera and veins stood before her. The headdress of vibrant quetzal feathers strapped around her forehead nearly reached the ceiling. Around her neck hung ropes of jade and turquoise. Her jugular beat in time with her heart. A long indigo cotton cloak with a gold clasp lay on her shoulders. It was a vision out of a nightmare, but Concepcion felt no fear. The black oily eyes felt kind. Iridescent swirls danced and smiled.

"Who are you?"

The woman's expression turned wounded. "Exactly. I am the forgotten woman in the shadows with no skin to show. My name is Mictecacíhuatl."

"The goddess?" Concepcion's eyes went large. She took

Mictecacíhuatl's hand and rose to her feet. "Why am I here? Where am I?"

The goddess paced the damp floor with her cloak dragging behind. Water dripped from the ceiling of jagged stalactites. Droplets floated in the opposite direction. Flaming torches poked from the walls. Concepcion thought she might be in a dream.

"You are in part of my home. A private place not even my husband is allowed to venture. And you are here because your sister has caught my attention. I am weary. I am angry. I am through with the shadows and stories. A change is due. A new cycle."

Concepcion looked down at her bare feet, which stood in a pool of warm water. "She's dead. I feel it."

"Yes. But I want her to live again. I will need your help."

Concepcion looked at the queen. "Anything. Tell me what I must do. Am I dead?"

"You are not dead but will not live as you would a normal life. All your life force will be used for the necessary energy to give Milagros a chance to be reborn when the time is right. A sacrifice is always required."

Concepcion knew this well. Life was a series of sacrifices, big and small. "Is this because we're different?"

"Yes. Your ancestors, your blood. I would like you to meet Ix Chel. She is one of my handmaidens even though she did not die in childbirth."

A woman who looked to be in her sixties emerged from the shadows. Her dark skin was the same shade as Concepcion's. She wore a brightly colored huipil that reminded Concepcion of the serape Milagros took with her when she left. This was matched with a plain white cotton skirt scraping her ankles.

"Hello and pleased to meet you." Concepcion gave her a smile and nodded.

Ix Chel reached beneath her huipil and extended an obsidian knife with a leather handle to Concepcion.

The queen took the knife and pressed the edge against a fingertip until a bead of blood gathered. She opened her palm and offered the knife to Concepcion. "Do you accept the offer to be the sacrifice? Carry this blade with you. You see, the power you and your sister had on earth came from Ix Chel, and now you will hold the blade and shall channel to Milagros."

Concepcion's mouth widened. Realization, wonder, and memory sped past her mind. She closed her eyes and smiled, feeling at home.

"I accept." She could feel the queen's bloody fingertip on her forehead and traveling down her nose, past her lips. Concepcion opened her eyes. The queen had stepped aside and Ix Chel stood in her place with clothing matching her own in her hands. Concepcion embraced her ancestor Ix Chel.

"Come sister, let us walk in the gardens and allow the queen to rest. She has many preparations. You can change into these new clothes."

Concepcion followed Ix Chel out of the cave through a tunnel and into blinding sunlight that felt wonderful on her skin. Her nose was filled with rose and lavender.

I am just the sacrifice.

★　★　★

Benny laid the notebook down. It was half memoir and half fairy tale. What the hell was any of it? Part of him wished he had never found it. The woman without the skin. His vision as a child. Could it be real? There was no way Concepcion could know of his experience. He shook his head then cradled it with his hands. *You are a doctor, dammit. Fucking straight A's in math and science. How?*

He was suddenly overcome with the desire to see Hector, feel Hector's arm around his shoulder and his head in the crook of his neck. Hector's kisses were the magic that was missing in his world. He was some brujo casting a spell of desire over him with those dark eyes. Not just desire, companionship. A meeting of two minds and hearts to share the weight of the world. Two accomplished brown gay men navigating the world. The only thing Benny ever wanted in life was to be a successful doctor. Now he wanted Hector to be part of that plan, if there was any plan to life.

CHAPTER NINE

"Belinda, you did a good thing here. It's beautiful. We have to put this up right away, take photos for Benny."

Hector held up the plaque to honor Milagros that arrived while we were in Mexico. I didn't spare any expense when I ordered it before we left. Milagros's name and birthdate were engraved at the top with the outline of a cicada below. Hector took out his tools to attach the bronze plaque to the ceiba tree.

"Put it here." I pointed to the spot with the worst of the scarred graffiti. Milagros would not be forgotten, now or ever. Instead of some terrible phantom, she would be known as the woman she was in life. Someone would have to regularly polish the bronze so that it would be legible forever. Hector drilled it into place, then joined me to see how it looked at a distance. It gave the tree and the spot a sense of significance. I wished I could scrub the tree or paint it a different color to hide the rest of the scars.

We invited the preacher to the tree to say a prayer at noon. Without hesitation he agreed. He had been there that day, and saw Milagros's dead body with his own eyes. When he arrived, he stopped short, looking forlorn and distant.

"It's beautiful, Belinda. I'll do my best to find the words to match this gift."

We held hands and bowed our heads in prayer. The insects chirped and sang with no other sound around us. As Pastor Rich spoke his voice cracked. He stammered, searching for the right thing to say. I could tell the vision of Milagros had lived with him every day of his life. How was anyone the same after that? We left in time to greet the new guests from the SyFy Channel, who were due at the farm for filming.

The crew of three, two men and one woman, showed up smelling like aired-out weed with glassy eyes. They were a bunch of kids who found IG video fame filming haunted places all over the US then given a show by the SyFy Channel. All three wore horror film t-shirts and ripped jeans that had probably been bought that way. Hector just wanted to get this obligation over with. His sleep didn't come easy, and when it did, it didn't last long. The trauma of Mexico was affecting him in ways I didn't dare to ask because I didn't want to admit that I wanted La Reina to make an appearance. My morbid fascination was only growing by the day, feeding something inside of me that had an endless appetite. I held so much sorrow for Milagros the woman, but the strangeness of it all captured my curiosity, numbing me to the fear and horror. Something else was at work. We were not terribly alone on this planet, resembling fruit left to rot in a bowl. The slow exsanguination was already being felt and seen around the world. I hated being alone more than anything.

The SyFy trio brought their own candles, black cloth with a white pentagram in the middle, sage and all the other things that would make for good, spooky TV.

"No one said anything about a séance or a Ouija board." Hector was sweating profusely while towering over a guy who looked young enough to be my son. His skin looked as oily as his scruffy hair.

"Look, man, it's not a big deal. It's a cheap piece of shit I bought on eBay and there really is nothing here. Lighten up. It's just a show. Plus, you've already been paid."

Hector knew he was defeated. He needed that money to get

him through the low season. Buying this property was a decision made with his heart instead of his brain wired for business. He'd invested his entire net worth in refurbishing and maintaining this farm. He brushed roughly against the guy they called Josh and the cameraman named Bo and went straight to his room. Josh continued setting up props with Maxine, the pretty young woman with hair dyed a shade too black. They kept the lighting to a minimum with candles so they could switch to night vision made famous by a certain sex tape made by a blonde socialite. Sex and tragedy sell.

I followed Hector to his room. "Hey, want to talk?" I asked through the closed door.

After a few seconds, Hector opened the door. His face was a mixture of anger, fear and exhaustion. The strong wide jaw looked jowlier and his eyelids hung lower than usual. He needed to sleep.

"I'm scared. I don't like this stuff. I've been around it all my life and I've tried to distance myself. It really creeps me out. My grandmother told me things in the past, how there's a line as fine as a mark drawn by a sharpened pencil that separates white and black magic. You know what determines that? Us. We are the magic we make, our intent, the way we manifest things. I'm so scared of making the wrong decision, of being part of that dark instead of the light. The things I've done in the past. Those bonuses on Wall Street don't come easy. Don't even get me started on my college days. Then after all that stuff in Mexico. The blood.... It was probably shock, but I swear that blood looked just like the lake near my home, Lake Catemaco, and their bodies were the mountains. I wanted to touch it. Am I a sick bastard or what?" His hands were wet with sweat when I reached out to clasp them. Why didn't I feel the same sense of dread?

"We've just experienced something traumatic. It's okay to be scared."

"You're not scared. You don't seem to be as freaked out by this."

That hurt. He could see the puncture he made into me.

"I'm sorry. That isn't what I meant. I don't know how you can handle yourself with all of this."

He was right. It was strange. Since arriving at the farm, I had felt somehow disembodied, a ghost that didn't know she had already died, but at first I took that for my self-loathing and depression. Now it was more like a journey of discovery. Inner knowledge. Dare I say peace?

"I don't know. I stopped trying to control things or figure it all out because all I do is fuck things up. And don't talk to me about college. I've probably fucked more guys than you. Let's go down and be part of this. Have some say in this. I've got money saved if you need to kick their weed-smoking, little punk asses out of here. I have your back."

If there was going to be a séance, Hector would be involved. We double-checked that the bathroom door was locked as per his grandmother's instructions. It was time to start the show. We took our places on the sofa away from the cameras as Maxine and Josh kneeled on either side of the coffee table in front of the lit fireplace that made the entire room uncomfortably warm. This would be aired during Halloween, so they insisted on the fire to add a sense of the season. Hector kept dabbing his face with a white handkerchief.

"Hey, everyone! Josh and Maxine are here with this vintage Ouija board in a house that has possessed true horror and a farm that is said to be cursed. Will we contact the spirit, or will it get to us first? They say La Reina de Las Chicharras was murdered here and is the new Bloody Mary."

Ugh, reality TV. I felt angry at their tone. I guess I expected them to treat this whole thing with a little more respect. Perhaps do some research on all aspects of the story. If it was up to me, I would have thrown them out for that shitty intro. Despite all I had seen in Mexico, I still didn't *really* believe anything supernatural would make an appearance. I wanted there to be, but realistically it was all just spooky coincidences. Did I get a strange sensation while standing over those dead bodies? Yes, but when I think back to it, it might have been mild shock.

Hector's hand shook as it squeezed mine when Maxine and Josh placed their fingertips on the planchette in the middle of the board. Before anything could happen with that cheap piece of cardboard, we heard a click, followed by the distinct sound of a door opening. The youngsters looked at each other and smiled. Hector jumped to his feet, mad as hell with an excuse to kick them out.

"All right, who's up there? I didn't give anyone permission to stage anything."

"Nobody, man! It's just the three of us." Josh locked eyes with the cameraman, then flicked his head towards the stairs as he rose to see where the noise was coming from.

"No! Don't go up there!" boomed Hector.

The young man bounded up the stairs before Hector or I had a chance to catch up. The cameraman dashed quickly behind. Before we reached the top step, we heard a loud crack followed by Josh's body falling from the top of the staircase. Maxine screamed. Hector rushed down the stairs. The cameraman kept filming, focusing on the body splayed on the floor in a broken, contorted shape of bone through skin. Josh's skull and mouth leaked blood, with chunks of brain matter splattered like a halo. Dead eyes fixed on the ceiling. The cameraman continued up the stairs and I followed behind, holding my stomach. I found this scene more frightening than the one in Mexico because I knew there wouldn't be a frail old woman at the top of the stairs.

"Who's there?" I demanded from the dark of the opened bathroom door.

Under the sound of the young woman screaming for someone

to call an ambulance, I could hear running water. I still had a small death wish when my emotions got the better of me. I needed to see. The cameraman filmed my back and the darkened room. He could have no part in this. I turned to him.

"Go to Maxine. You should care more about your friends." I could see the desire for internet fame in his eyes as he glanced at the room then back towards the stairs, but I wasn't about to have another body here. "Go, you asshole!" Fucking kids these days. He ran down the stairs to comfort Maxine while Hector paced back and forth on the phone near the body.

I put one foot in front of the other, ready to see something that would give me nightmares. Instead it was just an empty bathroom with the tub a quarter full of water. As I reached out to turn off the faucet, I could feel someone behind me. I knew it couldn't be anyone in the house because I could still hear their voices downstairs and the distant sound of sirens. Chicharras and moths pummeled their wings against my stomach lining, poisoning the acid that wanted to rise to my throat. I turned off the water. The door slammed behind me. I felt my way around to find the light switch. It didn't work. I was in a vortex of darkness. If my inner turmoil, my self-hate, could exist, it would look like this. Alone and not alone in the bathroom, I was standing in a place that looked how I felt on the inside, but I felt strangely relaxed in this dark box without light. I let go of my fear and remembered the first time I held my child in my arms with blood and vernix coating his face. It was the face of pure love that I'd somehow lost along the way on my journey of mistakes that I called life. It was a place I had to return to. What a nice last thought. I put myself in fate's hands. Surrendered.

I turned to confront whatever was there, even if it meant I'd be dead in an instant, like Josh. Something wet and sticky touched my cheek. A sharp point that could have been a knife or nail traced my jaw. I could tell any more pressure applied to my

flesh would cause real pain. My chest trembled. I didn't know
what was in here with me, in my weightless darkness.

"I can feel you want to die. Do you know how many souls
that reside with me would do anything for the life you live and
the life you have left to live? Poor Milagros never had a chance."

"You aren't Milagros?"

"No. I am the Queen of the Dead, Mictecacíhuatl. Milagros is
here with us. She is inside of me, growing stronger every day. For
years her name has been whispered here. For years she has fed on
the living, slowly and patiently so as not to attract attention. We,
the quiet women with a great rage on the verge of breaking loose
to be something else."

The sharp end and sticky padded flesh moved from my cheek
to my neck to my breast. It was comforting and even a bit sensual
and exciting. Death's touch was arousing because I had no fear of
it. Her voice had the smoothness of a stocking, with my curiosity
tightening around my mind like a garter.

"Your skin is so soft. The shade of brown is beautiful. You
should not hate it so even if you are made to believe it is not good
enough. That wickedness must end," she whispered.

I wanted to reach out and touch this manifestation of death,
this woman. Her power intoxicated me. The power was familiar.
That sensation filled me whenever I achieved what I set out to
accomplish before I dimmed my pride because I didn't think I
deserved it. From the tone of her voice, I knew she did not mean
to harm me. Josh didn't last this long before she discarded him.

"What do you want?" The question was tainted with the
thought of sex as she continued to knead my breast, the tip of her
sharp nail teasing my nipple. I wanted to know what all of this
meant. Who was I in all of this? Up to now I had seen three dead
bodies and none of it had fazed me in the least. Was I that dead
inside too?

"The gods only reveal their plans when it is the right time

for them. You really think this is all about you? Selfish child of a baby universe with so little knowledge of the things far from here." She moved her hand from my breast to between my legs. "Your purpose has always been there. You will know when the time comes."

I was fully aroused as I only wore a thin pair of leggings. The tip of her nail stroked the soft opening of my lips. I could not stifle my moan. The commotion downstairs and thundering footsteps scarcely registered. I reached out to touch death. Her flesh was warm and sticky, like the lubrication causing my clit to hum. I felt a hard, rounded mound that I think was her belly. I pulled my hand away as I felt it pulsate. Hector was trying to unlock the door while also hitting it as hard as he could.

"She needs to be fed, then she will be in this world again."

"Milagros? After all this time?"

"Yes. I will show you. May I kiss you?" Without answering, I leaned into her voice. Wet lips pressed against mine. She took my breath away with her tongue and I took a memory from her mouth with mine.

★   ★   ★

Milagros knew she was dead. Her body felt like wet papel picado, half-dissolved and soft with parts missing. The voice in her ear as she slipped away provided some relief that she didn't have to endure this degradation alone. Her pain was seen and heard. The promise of a half life was better than no life. What the voice wanted she did not know; however, the chance of vengeance honeyed the tears that wet her lips.

When her body was untethered, the rest of her, the part not seen by the human eye, sat on a sturdy branch of the place she would be bound to. Weariness in soul and the lead in her bones needed rest. Her head and right arm leaned against the trunk as she scanned the dead farm. From this vantage point she could watch the family slowly sell their belongings. It wasn't long before a body beneath a sheet was wheeled out of the home that would soon be abandoned. That was what she wanted. A radius of death, with her at the epicenter. Her tears might have been honey on her lips, but they were poison to this earth that had claimed her sweat for too long. There was concern for the workers who had to find employment elsewhere, but her people were strong. They would find a way with La Causa and warriors like Chavez to lead the way. If only she could have made it that far.

Even when all the perpetrators were gone, Milagros decided to stay put. There was no space she felt she belonged to in the borderless place of the spirits. When her mortal life was extinguished, all of her rage and resentment formed a tight ball, then exploded into supernova light with all the power that a heavenly body possesses. This brought her self-awareness back. This gave her the ability to follow the voice as she took vengeance with the unseen force as her guide. Having a second chance to reclaim her dignity felt good.

The last one was the sheriff.

★   ★   ★

It was during a hunting trip with his brother that she stalked the two in the trees, disorientating them with thrown stones and rustling leaves, making them think there was a big buck to be had. She led a beautiful creature to their sights, stroking its soft coat and majestic antlers, then she scared it away. Sheriff Don raised his rifle, licking his lips once, then stopped when a crack rang out, sending birds into flight. He looked down to see a hole through his flannel shirt. A black stain spread before his eyes. His own brother had shot him through the chest. He collapsed, hearing the distant shouts of his kin but unable to scream back.

His brother ran to his side, but the last face and voice the sheriff experienced was Milagros, who sat on a tree branch above his head. She pulled a red handkerchief from over her nose, down to her neck, then opened her mouth to allow blood to fall in long strings over his face. Her eyes, black marbles, reflected his death to him. The terror on his face was delicious, satiating her in a way that could only be matched by knowing Tanya was still imprisoned alive. The idea of turning the other cheek filled Milagros with bitterness, because it was difficult to do such a thing underfoot or dead.

With her vengeance complete, she didn't know what to do with herself or what purpose she served by lingering on.

People walked by, sensing her presence and sometimes seeing her. They looked directly at her, not knowing whether to continue to stare or run in terror. We are told ghosts don't exist, that horror is fiction. She could tell they didn't believe their eyes. Years passed without a feeding, the claiming of a life. No one wanted to live in the house or settle on the land. Good. Let it rot. The skin on her body slowly glued itself to the tree with the help of wasp nests and spiderwebs. All these creatures lived, gave birth, fed and died upon her body while she grew as wooden as the tree. Knowing life went on somewhere was reassuring. Milagros was sure her sister was no longer alive because she couldn't sense her.

Then one day the voice that once comforted her through her murder spoke again. The Queen sat next to Milagros. "My dear, your sadness has become an illness. How can you grow strong if you do not feed yourself?"

Milagros could only shift her eyes; she didn't want to disturb the creatures that had made a home on her body. "What else am I to do? I've been avenged."

The Queen stroked Milagros's hair, securing it behind her ear. "There is so much more. So much wrong in this place. You have a throne in this world and the next. Time, energy and the cosmos pump through invisible strings. These can be manipulated with the right force."

Out from the crook of Milagros's neck crawled the wasp queen, to pay her respects to another queen. Mictecacíhuatl took the wasp into her bloody hand. A smile crossed her wet, muscular face as the wasp queen scurried up her arm. "Your sister lives in between spaces. What if you could see her? Would that make you happy, give you the encouragement you need?"

Milagros's eyes glittered. "Is she okay? Can I see her? I thought she was dead."

"Come with me. It will hurt to move from this tree, but you must." Mictecacíhuatl took Milagros by the hand, squeezing it hard to give her confidence. "Pull yourself, cihuatl. Your complacency will only be a second death. You have sat idle on that tree long enough. Come see your sister."

"My sister?" Milagros would do anything to see her sister, endure any pain.

The place where the wasp's nests attached flesh to bark cracked and ripped. Milagros gritted her teeth as her skin pulled from muscle. Part of her scalp detached, revealing white skull. She held on to the Queen's hand to steady herself for the agony of detaching the rest of herself from the tree. It was time for her arms and hips. With a scream loud enough to scare the birds away, Milagros pulled the rest of her body from the tree.

Instead of falling face first into the dirt, she floated with Mictecacíhuatl.

"See, you can do it when you do not hide from who you really are. Follow me."

Milagros felt no pain despite knowing part of her skull was exposed. Then again, she was still dead. She followed the red woman, all muscle, organs, nails and teeth. Throbbing blue and red veins like writhing inchworms intertwined with muscle and bone, giving the illusion of living tattoos. Her eyes could suck you in with their depth. Once, Milagros's father took her to a cenote that was used for sacrifices and worship during the old times, before the land was seized by force. Portals to the divine are everywhere. It made her afraid because it wouldn't take much for her to dive in to see what waited below. The Queen's eyes were like that water. Necklaces of polished jade and turquoise hung around her neck, covering the fat of her breast. The fat deposits on her buttocks and thighs shook with every confident step. Flowing behind her was a cloak painted with scenes of their people like Milagros had seen carved at the temples of their ancestors. This woman was the most beautiful creature Milagros could imagine.

They entered the shell of a house sprayed with graffiti and littered with garbage. The floor was caked with a layer of animal droppings. Paint peeled off the walls, which were blackening from mold. The once immaculate home had become a ruin overtaken with rot, weeds and dust. Their destination was the bathroom where Betty died.

The small window was cracked and clouded over with a brown and green grime that matched the limescale-covered tub. A chipped white sink stood beneath a mirror that remained intact, without any blemish. It looked brand new, untouched by time or the elements.

Mictecacíhuatl positioned Milagros in front of the mirror and took her place behind. "I want you to see your heart's desire and source of sadness. Break your heart if you must, for it will be the only way through the realms of two worlds."

Milagros didn't want to break her heart, as she feared it would permanently remain shattered, but she wanted to see Concepcion, and maybe someone else.

The Queen lifted Milagros's arm towards the mirror so she could lay her palm against her reflection. She then exhaled hot breath over the surface of the mirror, fogging it.

"Milagros."

Milagros's eyes opened wildly. She knew that voice.

"Concepcion! Is it really you? Please? Let me see you!"

When the fog cleared, Concepcion's palms touched on the other side of the mirror. Both women laughed, with tears spilling from matching eyes. Two faces, one bloodline. Concepcion and Milagros appeared as they were on the day of Milagros's departure.

"I miss you, Concepcion. I'm sorry I never saw you again."

"Sorry! Why are you sorry? You have done nothing. But listen to me. There is a way, a way I have sacrificed my life for. You must feed. You must be reborn. It is the only way to save us all in the end."

"I'm nobody. I'm a girl from a village."

"Every single life has a purpose. You need to take your place. For me. For Mariposa."

Milagros's smile fled like the fog.

"I don't want to hear her name. It hurts too much."

The Queen nodded to Concepcion.

"Milagros, I have to go now, but please, take your place in this world. Goodbye and I love you. We will see each other again. I promise."

Milagros's hand slipped from the mirror once the image of her sister was gone.

The Queen placed both hands on Milagros's shoulders to comfort her as she sobbed.

"A breaking heart isn't just in the mind. It is also manifested physically, I know. You can't even begin to understand the pain I have endured each time my sternum has been cracked in two while the blood of our people coated the thirsty earth, sucked down so deep it trickled and spilled down my walls. The bones of my home are stained red and forever it will remain that way."

Milagros looked into the mirror again. "Mariposa. Can I see her?"

Mictecacíhuatl wrapped one arm around Milagros's waist.

"I know you have only experienced love, physical love, with one person: Mariposa. She is gone, as all humans die in old age. Her spirit is in the underworld, so you may not see her, but she looked for you upon her arrival. She was pleased to know there are big plans for you. What if I told you you could have another chance? At the time your love was forbidden, but it will not always be so. What if I told you Mariposa can also be a monarch by your side? Feed. Be reborn with me in flesh. This civilization will decay in time, and not by the will of the gods. By human will. Together we will begin again."

"I don't understand." Milagros searched her memory of old stories, both indigenous and those of the Bible.

"Tell me, my daughter Milagros, of your dearest memory of Mariposa."

Milagros shook her head. "No! It hurts too bad!"

"Touch the mirror and show me."

Milagros lifted a finger and placed it on the mirror.

"We knew we wanted each other when we first kneeled side by side while lighting candles for La Virgen. By chance our fingers touched. Our shoulders pressed together as we prayed, the sound of the choir practicing a cappella in the distance filled the vestibule. We met three times a week at the feet of La Virgen, just to be close to each other. I remember praying so hard to La Virgen to make it right so we could be together, to bless us and accept us. Just being by her side made me happy. In the dark no one could see our legs touching, just two pious girls at prayer, not in love, passing notes to each other."

The thought of Mariposa made Milagros want to turn and run as she too could feel her sternum cracking with a searing pain throbbing from the wound. That was her love.

It was the memory of their last encounter on Dia de Los Muertos that hurt most of all.

The village buzzed and everyone was busy with the festivities that gave them the opportunity to remain in Mariposa's room to consummate their desire. Mariposa claimed to have cramps to excuse her from traveling with her family to pay homage to their ancestors. Concepcion made an excuse for Milagros.

"She has a fever that will only get worse if we do not pray hard tonight." Their parents always listened to the wise-beyond-her-years Concepcion.

Milagros walked quickly through the streets with her shawl over her head and eyes down. She and Mariposa would have a mere three hours alone. Mariposa pulled her to her room, closed the shutters and locked the bedroom door. She lit candles with trembling hands and with that same uncertain touch she reached for Milagros's waist then brushed her fingertips along the side of her thighs as they crept above her knee-length dress. Their mouths met; their bodies a perfect fit. The tender flesh between Mariposa's legs in the candlelight was as beautiful as the black lace mantilla she wore on her head during mass. It bent to the will of her tongue and mouth. The softness of her body was a delight that only the gods could have created as it shivered with every nibble and lick.

The night was beautiful but fleeting, just like the shockwaves of her orgasm as she looked into Mariposa's perfect brown eyes. Her slick fingertips gently rocked back and forth as she cried out in pleasure. Sweat the size of rosary beads rolled down her neck and between her breasts. It lasted beyond human understanding of time, yet not long enough. When the sensation of love wore off, she knew there was no way they could get away with being together. That was her first taste of the cruelty of the world. The last was her death without seeing Mariposa, or her family, again.

Sadness stirred, it thickened and boiled and hardened until it was fury. Milagros slowly lifted her eyes to the mirror, looking directly at the Queen.

"Tell me. Show me how to have another chance with Mariposa and my sister at my side."

Mictecacíhuatl's lips curled to a wicked smile. She narrowed her eyes. She lifted both hands above Milagros's head and clacked her nails together. Cicadas fluttered through the crack in the window. Their song took on a high-pitched tone like they were speaking to each other. They flew in a circular tornado until they created a ring around Milagros's head, laying their bodies down, connecting their legs to one another, their wings stitching into her hair. Soon they stopped their hymn and movement as their bodies transformed to gold.

"Every queen deserves a crown. Take your place, La Reina de Las Chicharras."

Milagros lifted her chin with the same defiance she felt before the incident that made her leave her town. "I am ready."

The women left the dilapidated house with the intention of claiming this world for their own. La Reina de Las Chicharras was born, and she was hungry. But only those in south Texas knew the stories. For now.

*   *   *

The lights flickered on and Hector burst through the door, crashing into me. "Are you okay? What the hell happened? The police are here." I knew this encounter was real because Hector was looking at me with bewilderment. "There's blood all over you! What the fuck?"

"She won't hurt us. I think we're in her plans," I said excitedly, forgetting another death had occurred at the farm. But we weren't alone. I wasn't alone. Milagros was not alone in her death. I said a prayer of thanks in my mind.

*   *   *

The suspicious police questioned me until the video showed there was no way I could have killed the SyFy guy. I told them I didn't know what happened or why there was blood on me. The two officers looked on edge when it was time to investigate the bathroom.

I could hear them whispering, "It's like that damn urban legend, La Reina. Fuck. I thought that was just sleepover or messing-around-after-school shit."

"Yeah, I know! I wrote a damn paper in college about unsolved true crime. This is some freaky bullshit I do not get paid enough for."

Their conversation shifted to me.

"This chick looks possessed or like she just danced with the Devil. Blood all over. Fucking hell."

It was three in the morning when the police left, calling the incident a stunt gone wrong. Maxine and Bo insisted Josh never mentioned a prank, but it wasn't the first time they bent the rules for ratings. Perhaps he didn't say anything so it would appear authentic.

Hector didn't want to stay in the house; he was frantic. He was ready to abandon it, another dream, another baby that was not meant to be. I didn't tell him I didn't want to leave if the Queen was here, so I offered to stay and keep an eye on the place if he wanted to move into a motel in town or go visit friends in New York. His anger at the disappointments in his life changed his mind. And it seemed death was following him. He decided to dig his heels into this poisoned ground and stay. We both showered off our sweat, and I the blood, after closing off the living room where Josh died. Neither of us wanted to be alone, so we camped out on his bedroom floor. Most people would have gone to bed, but Hector pulled out the whiskey, knowing I wasn't going to let him drink alone, preach or tell him it would all be okay. I'm a woman of a certain age. I know that shit isn't always right.

"Shall we toast to death?" He looked as old as the preacher in his weary sorrow as he raised his glass.

"Let's toast to life because we're still here. Death needs us for some reason," I countered.

We tossed back our whiskeys then he poured us another. It burned good.

"You want to hear a scary story?"

I stopped with the shot glass at my lips, remembering the other slumber party, the very beginning of the story we were living. "You know it was in a very similar situation I first heard about Milagros."

Another shot at the same time. "I'm gonna tell you why all this is scaring the shit out of me."

Hector told me he never liked the family business or their reputation as powerful brujos. It was his sister, Marie, who held a deep interest. Hector liked books, math, things he could see and touch in the real world. Every change in season his family would gather at Lake Catemaco to pray, give offerings to the spirits and remember family members who had passed. His uncle tried to teach him how to swim in that lake, but something felt so wild, out of control, in that deep water. Hector did not like things to be out of control or displaced. He preferred order, and there's no order when it comes to the spirits or water so deep you can't touch the bottom.

The spirits almost claimed his father when Hector was ten years old. A woman from the neighborhood showed up at the house. She wore chunky gold earrings that dangled heavily, a matching thick gold necklace and rings on both hands. Her nails were long and red, squared at the tips. She chewed her red lips and wiped her eyes when Hector answered the door. This visitor was expected, so Hector let her in. Her husband died suddenly, but she knew he left money for the family. He always said if he were to die without cause, they would be taken care of. Unfortunately, he failed to disclose the details. Without knowing where their cash and valuables were hidden, the family would starve, she pleaded.

Hector's father, Hidalgo, sister, grandmother and uncle were all present at the ceremony, seated in one of the bedrooms converted to his father's study. Of course, Hector had to be there. Marie had her arms folded and glared at him.

Earlier that day she whined, "But I want to learn, Papa! Hector doesn't know anything about our family. He just likes school." Hidalgo continued to prepare the candles and sweep the floor before the ceremony.

"Marie, you will have your day," their father replied. "But this is for us, the heirs of magic. It is how it has always been done in the family."

The only illumination in the room came from white and red candles, with all the windows covered. Freshly dusted statues of various saints in different sizes stood behind them, keeping watch with their hands together in pious prayer. Hidalgo wore a white guayabera with a black rosary around his neck. He closed his eyes and parted his lips while holding a watch owned by the dead man. Hidalgo swayed as he tried to conjure the spirit, his lips moving without sound. Suddenly he grimaced in an unnatural way, with his eyes protruding and mouth widening so tight around his teeth it appeared it might split at the corners. He clutched his chest and fell backwards. Ramon caught his brother mid-air then laid him down flat on the floor. A voice not belonging to Hidalgo spoke. It was like an echo in a canyon, if that sound could be at the level of a whisper.

"Blood money is not meant to be found. Blood money should be forever lost. You can have the gold but at a cost. Death."

The woman screamed. "Tell me! Tell me where it is! I don't care what my husband did. I had no part in it."

Hector's father's mouth turned into a wide grin. The flickering light made his teeth appear like sharpened spears and his eyes nothing but black shadow.

"Very well. It is underneath Pancho's house. I warned you. Your husband was a thief and worse. Many suffered from that money. Flesh money."

Hidalgo took a gasp of air and wrapped his fingers around his neck. His face was turning dark blue. Ramon shoved Hector to the side to give his brother mouth to mouth. Hector couldn't understand how Ramon and Marie could remain calm. Hidalgo sputtered before taking another breath and opening his eyes. He turned to Hector, who was in tears in the corner of the room.

"Don't be scared, mijo. Our power comes at a cost, but it is our birthright."

The woman who came for help had already left.

Marie got up from her seat and stood over her brother, then looked at her uncle and father. "See, he doesn't deserve or want to be by your side."

A week later, Hector heard the entire family of that woman and the deceased man was slaughtered by gangsters. Pancho was their family dog. He was the only one that survived and was adopted by the neighbors. It turned out the father was a hitman. The incident only made Marie more intrigued, while it served to push Hector even further from their gifts. He told himself it wasn't real, just theatrics and coincidences. He would rather think his father was a con man than a conduit for the spirits, something uncontrollable and in the realm of the unseen.

When Hector was fifteen, it was his grandmother who gave him the courage to tell his father not only did he not want to be a curandero, but that he was gay. His father didn't speak to him for a week but came around after praying. He had a dream that his son was a source of light. Just like people don't understand their ways, he might not understand his son's sexuality, but he wouldn't judge him. Hector would always be his son, his blood. Ramon was a harder sell. It wasn't until Ramon met his wife that he gave his nephew a hug for the first time in years.

Hector felt free to pursue his degree in math and business studies now that he had been honest with his family. Although he didn't take an interest in the magic side, he relished helping with the business of magic. Magic was lucrative. He kept detailed books about what was selling and what was not, inventory, best clients, peak sales times. Hector left nothing to chance or prayer. He showed his mother everything he did because he knew he wouldn't be there forever. New York City and tailored suits were his dreams. It was only a matter of time before he attained his dream, and he was willing to do anything to get there. Hector began running things, and soon the little business became big enough to pay for his education. After graduating from National Autonomous University of Mexico, he was accepted to Harvard Business School. New York City was next.

Hector was tipsy and feeling nice when he finished his story. His eyes looked heavy from exhaustion and booze. We blacked out next to each other in front of that Ouija board that didn't move once despite our trying it for half an hour. Piece of shit.

CHAPTER TEN

Tanya's body aged slower than she ever imagined was humanly possible. She lived her entire life in a bed, alert and aware of everything so acutely she wondered if her body possessed superhuman senses. During her twenties she saw a few visitors, mostly family. She hated every visit. They would plant themselves at her bedside, telling her how everyone was doing, dish all the local gossip – there was always ample gossip – inform her of what they were up to. No one seemed to get the sense that maybe she didn't want any more reminders that she couldn't do anything but listen and watch. There was also the way they looked at her, the pity in their eyes that made her want to poke them out with her thumbs.

Her thirties were left mostly alone, with her only company being the staff. They were nice enough, she supposed, but they gossiped to each other in front of her as if she was deaf, too. More stories of people living their lives in a world that continued to turn just fine without her in it. Her mother looked more bent over and wrinkled at every visit. Her breath and clothes reeked of cigarette smoke and perfume. Yellowed fingernails held Tanya's hand, but Tanya couldn't snatch it away or feel it. With nicotine- and coffee-stained teeth, her mother's smile was more of a sneer. She visited as much as possible, but the frequency was less and less. This absence wasn't that bad considering she loathed her mother by this time. There were always small digs about money being tight, and if only her daddy were here, and how terrible it was to drive over an hour to and from this care home. There was no money or desire to relocate. Tanya felt like a breathing bag of flesh that was a burden to her family. The worst part was she couldn't kill herself.

In her forties, someone came to inform her Momma was dead. A stroke as she stood in line for a bottle of vodka. No parents, no siblings and cousins had stopped coming around in her twenties. There was no one. The money left to her only lasted until her forty-eighth birthday. She had to move from private care to one paid for by the government. It smelled of urine, Pine-Sol and death. The only form of entertainment was watching a water stain in the ceiling grow larger, or guessing where the next chip of paint would peel away. There were more bed sores here because they would sometimes forget to wash her regularly. She could smell the rot and shit that excreted from her body as flesh and linen stitched together. Perhaps she would die soon.

Luck was not on her side, because, now in her eighties, she was still there. Shit, sores, rot, peeling paint. The only one who was on her side and never spoke a single word to annoy her was the preacher. He came once a month and just sat there, reading out loud from his Bible. Before leaving, he would say a short prayer. That was it. His presence was the only calming force in her life. She wondered what she ever did to deserve that, because no matter how hard she tried, the hate that bred inside never managed to subside. The stories and passages of the word of God touched no part of her. He never said it, but she could see in his eyes he was waiting for her to relent, to repent and soften. Never.

In all this time she never saw Milagros again. There were times the idea that this was all in her imagination played like fantasy, until one night she heard a click from the door. She couldn't move her head sideways to see what or who was creating the squelch of wet footsteps or the rhythmic thump that could only be a heartbeat. The steady dull boom reminded her of when she would lie on Billy's chest after sex. But this presence did not feel human. Tanya said a prayer in her mind until a bloody, skinless face appeared overhead. The thing's black eyes had the sheen of wet asphalt that only reflected Tanya's white hair and wrinkled face, which had the appearance of a finger left in water too long. After all those years of nothing but time to think, she didn't regret a moment of what she did.

"I have come for you. Milagros will now feed on your soul. I know you have wished for this for a very long time. If she didn't need your energy, you would be here until the sun devours your planet. You don't deserve anything less."

The Queen pulled the breathing tube out of Tanya's mouth with one fist and smashed the machine with the other before it could alert the staff to an emergency. Sparks flew into the air, sizzling as they landed on Tanya's face. Tanya gasped for air; her body seized. The Queen placed her lips over Tanya's, sucking out every molecule of oxygen in her lungs. Tanya's eyes bulged out of sockets that were turning black while the rest of her face went blue. Blood vessels popped in her eyes and leaked into the whites. She was helpless. The pain was unbearable, yet she was conscious for every second. Her very soul was being ripped apart into little pieces until it didn't exist. Her vision went black and then there was nothing. Death. The Queen looked upon the corpse in disgust.

"And now something for me." She extended her claw-like hand tipped with almond-shaped nails the color of iridescent pearls and the sharpness of a jaguar's tooth, then thrust it through the sternum of the dead body. Tanya's heart was in her grasp. The Queen raised it towards the ceiling, squeezing it like a saturated sponge. As the blood ran down her arm, the heart shrank and hardened until it was a lump of turquoise. She inspected the stone before using her index fingernail to create a hole through the center, then removed her necklace of jade. The heart would be placed around her neck for safe keeping until it would be bequeathed to her daughter. One soul extinguished from this world before another was reborn.

★ ★ ★

We awoke to a knock on the front door. Hector squeezed his eyes shut and moaned, turning over on his blanket and food wrappers. When did we even bring down the comforter from the bed? I felt dehydrated and needed to pee, so I forced myself off the floor. The knocking persisted the entire walk to the entryway. Through the stained-glass window in the center of the door, I could see it was the preacher. I felt sorry that he had to see my face or smell my breath after the night we had of booze and what looked like all the bags of chips in the kitchen.

He looked older than before. The bottom half of his face was covered in white, patchy stubble. His blue eyes were bloodshot with puffy eyelids hanging low, yet he took the time to comb down the remaining strands of silver hair and plaster it with something that shined.

"I'm sorry to disturb you, but I thought you would want to know that Tanya died last night."

This wasn't the news I'd been expecting. To be honest, I didn't care. "Okay. Thanks for the information. I'm not sorry to hear that. Why tell us?"

He shrugged, and didn't look me in the eye. "I don't know. You're still involved with this. They told me her tube was removed from her mouth and her heart torn from her body. Authorities think it might be someone trading in organs and others say it's witchcraft. Thought you should know."

"Thank you. And it was very kind of you for being there all these years. Do you want to come in for coffee?" I assumed that was the kind of thing to say to a man of God, far from what my heathen ass was thinking. Good fucking riddance to her. Unlike the dinosaurs that did nothing malicious, sometimes our capacity for cruelty made me think humans deserved the biggest asteroid in space to come crashing down on our no-good existence.

Pastor Rich waved me off. "No, no. There are people at the church wanting to talk to me. I have no idea about what. I'll see you all later." He shuffled off to his blue Toyota truck.

I heard a flush, then Hector walked down the stairs. "Who was that?"

"The preacher. He said Tanya is dead. Shall we celebrate with coffee?" Coffee from his fancy machine was all I could think about.

He rolled his eyes and grabbed a bag of beans for grinding. "I wish I had something nice to say, but I don't. Justice has been served."

Phones clogged with missed calls and messages alerted us that everything had changed. Even Veronica pulled herself away from the lobster beach barbecues to see if I was all right. The demise of the SyFy guy went viral. Maxine and the cameraman live-tweeted and IG videoed everything. Fucking kids. As Hector and I ate and drank on the floor, forgetting cell phones or the internet existed because we had lived during a time when they didn't, we were trending. By noon, media trucks were pulling up to the property. My son called with more questions than he had asked in months; all his friends were following the story. Poor preacher was getting accosted because someone let it be known that an old woman tied to the murder in 1952 died the same night in a most gruesome way. But the old man did the respectable thing and directed them to the tree. "Her name was Milagros Santos. That's all I will say."

Speculation surrounding the events kept popping up. Everyone had their own version of what caused Josh's death. By nightfall, 'the La Reina Challenge' was set up. People filmed themselves in front of all kinds of mirrors, Ouija boards, or pentagrams with candles, and called out her name. It didn't matter that nothing bad happened to anyone, with the exception of a few people who were claiming to have seen their deaths, swearing the experience was too real to be a dream or nightmare. Those unfortunate souls were dog-piled with all kinds of ridicule and vitriol. Anyone in the public eye who recounted their death experiences were accused of attention-seeking. Religious folks said it was the beginning of a new cult that was led by the Devil and just another sign of the end of days. I believed it because I *knew* she was real, but I didn't know the extent of her power or where she came from.

I returned my son's call, begging him not to do the challenge. He must have heard the fear in my voice, because he promised. Not that a teenager's promises often meant anything. Mine didn't. All I knew is that I didn't want him to see his death. What kind of choices would he make if he did? When I thought of my own death, it made me re-examine the capacity of cruelty I had for myself. I needed to fill that space with love. Let it spill over even when it hurt.

The Queen was out there, but not yet known. There was a legend that could be true, La Reina de Las Chicharras, Milagros, the woman of the field reaping souls. The story was taking on a life all its own, globally, hour by hour. She was collecting followers, and isn't that what matters? Hector's family from Mexico called, giving him different prayers for protection. He should pray to Mictecacíhuatl and La Virgen. I could hear the impatience in his voice growing with every phone call from Mexico. Who was I to tell them the Queen and Milagros were one? In that dark bathroom without light, we were a trinity in a tiny confessional. I kept that blasphemous thought to myself.

Then Hector received a call I imagined might come at some point. He stared at the number for a few rings, then answered it while looking at me. I wanted to shake my head to give him the courage to hang up, but this was something he had to do. His face changed the longer he listened, like a secret revealed to him.

"You are so full of shit. Excuse me, full of *yourself*," Hector said. "I can't believe I thought you should be the father of my child. Fuck off."

He hung up. His entire demeanor transformed in an instant. Whatever stagnant plume of toxic ectoplasm had been lingering from his past relationship vanished. He was communicating with Benny, but kept him at a distance. I wondered if that might change now.

"That bastard wanted to make money off me. Can you believe it? He was trying to pitch me an idea to use our past. After all those hurtful things he said, the cheating, the lies. Why did I not see him for what he really was? A fuck boy."

I did the only thing I could. I took him into my arms and told him I loved him. There was a real love for him that wasn't anything beyond care for another human who was trying to figure it all out like me. We weren't alone in this world. None of us was, just like no one was safe.

★   ★   ★

Hector finally agreed to give one informal tour and interview to a local station from San Antonio with the promise it wouldn't be made into a big production. He knew he couldn't hide forever and needed the money because the B&B would be closed indefinitely. All the deposits for upcoming events had to be returned. They wanted to interview me as well, but I refused. I was there to support my friend, plus I didn't want to speak of my experience with the woman in the dark room. We invited Pastor Rich over because Hector thought it might help ward off evil. Pastor Rich eagerly accepted the invitation. He had been there from the beginning and I suspected this talk of the supernatural had captured his curiosity. After all, he had dedicated his life to something that is not seen and not always felt, either.

The crew followed Hector and Monica Cortez, a journalist from KSAT14, up the stairs.

"And you said this is the bathroom where the original owner died?"

Hector nodded, then proceeded to open the unlocked door. It refused to budge. With a tight grip and a nervous smile, he twisted the doorknob back and forth, used the keys, but the door would not open. He pressed against it with his body, which was substantial in muscle and height. His eyes yelled for help when he looked at me as if he could sense something was about to happen, something that might change the world if that door opened.

Then I heard her. It was a sound as deep and hypnotic as the incantations of Buddhist monks in Nepal seeking enlightenment through sound. I remembered her touch and how good it felt, the warmth and wetness of her body next to mine. I approached the door, forgetting the cameras. The door banged open, hitting the wall. A black mass of chicharras, moths, flies and other types of insects with wings flew out of the bathroom. Everyone ducked and screamed except me. The insects tangled in my hair and whipped against my face as they struggled to free themselves. The cameraman continued to point the lens at the open door as the swarm flew around the house in a chaotic dance they made their own music to. The buzz of their different sounds was a choir not of this earth. She did not show her face, but the camera caught those shiny, black obsidian eyes that could be moonlight on a body of water at midnight. It also captured her voice. That voice was inviting, yet powerful. Stockings and garters with a stiletto heel and pointed tip. You wanted to know more, see whatever was there.

"We are here. And I am real. Mictecacíhuatl is my name. I am here for you all. Milagros will save you all."

Hector reached for the voice as he ducked from the insect horde. Monica ran down the stairs, almost tripping over her heels, and out the front door, releasing the insects into the atmosphere. I rushed into the bathroom to catch a glimpse of her, Mictecacíhuatl, but she was gone. I fell to my knees next to Hector, who stared into the dark room with an open mouth, eyes no longer yelling. He crossed himself and prayed. I asked Hector what he thought. With tears streaming down his face, he took me into a tight embrace.

"She said, 'You will have your child. I accept you, my son.'" Hector pulled himself from the floor, helping me up in the process. "I never thought I would be a believer, but I am now. All those years I doubted, cursed the family's so-called gift."

This new entity was offering the one thing people crave beyond riches – acceptance. This new entity made herself known. The video had gone viral by the evening. How could it not? Imagine if the lives of Jesus, Mohammed, Santa Claus, Confucius and Buddha all had the benefit of technology. Faith would have taken on a whole new meaning.

★   ★   ★

The crickets and chicharras around the house were loud, louder than I ever remember insects capable of sounding. Then again, I had lived in Philadelphia for years. You don't hear much except sirens, buses and cars. The city sounds are mechanical, jarring, unnatural.

The tree where Milagros died became an experience. It grew, extending the shade it offered, with the leaves taking on a vibrant green. The scarred base smoothed out the lashings over time. Humans, animals and insects found themselves drawn to its roots and branches. People brought benches to the tree where they could sit and talk to others, complete strangers. Or just listen to the chicharras' song and chirping of life. The busiest times were sunrise and sunset. No matter the advances in science or technology, the sun remains a powerful sight, like the ocean.

Five feet deep surrounding the tree was a quilt of candles and flowers in all states of freshness and decay. Some people left photos of young women who were taken too soon from this world. Their own Milagroses. The crowd was eclectic; however, if pushed for a description, I would say they were the ones on the fringes. The ones who didn't fit into an exact box. They wanted to believe in something different because the world was in a state of stage four cancer and no one could see a way back. There was no chemo for what we had, and it was cutting it close to the point of no return. The marginalized sought out their Queen with the privilege of having no skin to hold her back. Her power was raw. From the stars.

Two camps developed online: one tried to explain why the insects might be so loud this time of year and why the farm's soil had been rendered useless since the murder of Milagros. The increasing amount of people claiming to have seen their deaths was discounted as mass hysteria, a fad. Even when a portion of them changed different aspects of their lives based on their death experiences, including spreading the good word of this new queen, they were not believed.

There was also the political relevance of this place. It should be revered for its symbolism even if it didn't hold anything supernatural. Hate is not an idea or a thing in the sky. Hate is spilled blood with the stench of putrefying flesh that should never leave our memory. It should be burned and laid to rest. But for some, hate is the only way they can feel comfortable with what they don't understand or can't control.

Then there were the believers: the people who prayed and lit candles at the ceiba tree. They called on Milagros, La Virgen and Mictecacíhuatl. Poems were written. The stories of the Aztecs were revived, as were all the stories of those civilizations plundered and left to die. Mexico struggled to cope with the surge in global tourism that gave the country a boost for its citizens. Old superstitions die hard, and people were really worried the voice would come for them if pilgrims wanting to learn more about Mictecacíhuatl were harmed. The tree was a place of worship, a place of past scars that had not healed yet hope that they would. This was a place between the light and the dark. There were no other deaths, just viral worship. The Queen of the Dead was making a comeback.

Hector and I watched the video at least ten times. We couldn't explain away our experiences. Marie sent a box full of books, herbs, oils and candles at Hector's request for the first time in his life. Marie did not hesitate to send it. She wanted to visit, to see for herself, but he warned her off, just in case this wasn't a benevolent force. Marie had two children at home who needed her.

Hector sat at the kitchen table, reading books recommended by his sister on the history of curanderos and their practices. He looked like a student preparing for finals. The world was changing, and we had to change with it. More people wanted to venture into the house to see if the phenomenon was true, but it remained closed. The governor of Texas was allowed to use army reserves to keep a perimeter around the house to avoid vandals or intruders.

Both of our past lives were getting pulled into the narrative of La Reina de Las Chicharras. Thank God the worst of it was during the Triassic No Social Media Era. If there was no post, did it really happen? My son was beginning to worry. We Skyped regularly, as he was following every bit of information about this new goddess that wasn't so new. He told me I should keep a video diary or write everything down. His curiosity scared me, but it brought him closer to me. I cherished every call that went from minutes to hours. Now he wanted to take that trip. He wanted to explore his Mexican roots. I gave him a list of books to read for discussion on our next chat. This boy was not a reader in the slightest, but he jumped at the chance. His friends were saying I was a bit of a celebrity. I guess I was, considering I didn't really do anything of merit except be at a place and time where things were happening. Dumb luck. At least, I thought it was.

Then, after watching an interview, Hector had an idea that would change our lives forever. It was a man slightly older than us, Dave Bradford. He was born and raised in Alice but left as soon as he turned eighteen and never returned. We watched his story along with millions of others around the world.

★   ★   ★

It started with a group of boys in 1985: Dave, Marcus and Fernando ventured out to the farm as a dare on Halloween night. The sped on their bikes through the darkness, but had to hop off once they reached the edge of the farm. The grass was impossible to navigate in its wild overgrowth. Before entering, they stopped to look at the decrepit house with the outline of the spire piercing the full moon. Marcus took out a flashlight from his backpack. The tube of light shone brightly at the door, which appeared open.

"If this bitch is real, I want to see her," remarked Fernando.

"Pass the fucking pipe. I need a hit before we do this." Marcus pulled out a palm-sized glass bong, put it to his lips, and inhaled deeply.

Dave looked at the house, feeling uneasy as his friends moved towards the door. He placed a headlamp that had been tucked in his back pocket around his forehead. With ease the door creaked wide open. Dave looked from side to side to inspect the surroundings. There was something heavy about this place, and it stunk. "Let's just do it and go."

"All right, Davey boy. Say it first! Don't be a pussy!"

Fernando and Marcus laughed in a cloud of suffocating weed smoke that was a welcome change of smell from piss and animal shit.

"La Reina de Las Chicharras. Is that right, Fernando? You're Mexican. Not me."

"You know I don't speak Spanish," Fernando said as he tried not to exhale the smoke from another hit of the bong.

Marcus took another deep hit. "La Reina de Las Chicharras! Chicharrachicharrachicharra. I got an A in Spanish last report card."

The house was silent for a few seconds while they waited for something to happen. Then the three burst into laughter.

"Give me that." Dave grabbed the bong from Marcus, feeling stupid for allowing his grandparents' tales of the farm to get to him. His great uncle made deliveries here and said he witnessed things he didn't believe were real. And so much death. The land was dead. Those stories kept Dave up for weeks. It was nothing after all. Before he could bring the bong to his lips, the creaking sound of a door could be heard above their heads. Marcus turned the flashlight to the noise and Dave whipped his head in the same direction. Both beams of light caught the figure at the top of the stairs.

"You called?"

The three teens gawked, not believing what they were seeing with their own eyes. They were high. This couldn't be real. There stood a woman in tattered clothing stained with blood that oozed from her neck. A chunk of scalp could be seen missing. Her skin looked speckled in red and purple raised welts. Dave couldn't tell if it was the darkness or if her eyes were really that black. It was the kind of black that had no end, like death. The boys stood motionless. Marcus thought someone was dressed up for Halloween, doing the same as them, or it was the weed.

"Holy shit, guys. Are you s–seeing this?" he stammered.

Dave and Fernando wordlessly nodded.

"You called for me? Hear my name, Milagros! La Reina de Las Chicharras." Her jaw unhinged, releasing wasps, flies, hornets, and cicadas into the house. The buzz increased as they jerked in different directions in a black cloud, surrounding the boys without stinging. "Tell them you saw me! We are here!"

The three screamed in unison, scrambled out of the house and into the fields then scattered towards their homes on their bikes. With the other boys gone, Dave pumped his arms hard as he ran to his bike. He allowed tears to stream from the corners of his eyes.

It's real. Holy shit, it's real! he kept repeating to himself as he pedaled home.

When he saw the light of his front porch, he ditched the bike and ran into his house directly to his bedroom, ignoring his family. He slept in his clothes with the lights on and the sheet tucked all the way to his chin.

The following day at school, the boys met up during first-period break. Not one had slept.

"Dude, what happened? Did I imagine that?"

"It was real. We've smoked that bag of weed before. There's nothing extra in it. I saw her! Heard her!"

"Heard what, you nerds?" Candice Gonzalez leaned against the locker with Mary Freeman. Usually the boys got all cocky when they were around, but not today. Today they looked like they did in elementary school before a test, but also like they rolled out of bed without a shower or brushing their teeth before school.

Dave was the first to speak. "Look into a mirror and say, 'La Reina de Las Chicharras. Chicharrachicharrachicharra.' See what happens."

Mary rolled her eyes. "I've done Bloody Mary and nothing happens. Nice try, assholes. Halloween was yesterday. Come on, Candice."

Candice watched the ashen-faced boys still huddled together like frightened children, talking low so no one could hear. She had heard stories about a haunted farm. How could she ever escape the tales of La Llorona? She would try it with Mary and Linda tonight. Probably nothing would happen.

CHAPTER ELEVEN

"If I want to try something, will you hear me out? I did it when I was in New York and if I didn't do it, I would probably still be with Tom. I can only imagine the anger I would harbor towards him, and myself, if I didn't find the courage to tell him what I really wanted and needed in our relationship. I didn't tell my family about it because they would have badgered me to do it in Mexico, or tell me they know a guy who knows a guy who can bless the damn bag of fungus. I wanted an unbiased experience. We should try to reach out to her. Maybe we can breach the border of our worlds."

Hector pulled out a bag of shriveled mushrooms and waved it in the air. "I know they look like a bag of gross dicks and smell just as bad as a high school gym locker room, but these are strong, stronger than what you'll find in Amsterdam, or anywhere else I'm told."

I snatched the bag away, laughing. It made me think of the time I first tried mushrooms. The party kind, nothing blessed. Broke as hell, I don't know how my friend and I got hold of them. Maybe someone I fucked. We sat in the chain coffee shop with Americanos in front of us. The flaky dried hallucinogenic meal went down easy with a mouthful of coffee. Minutes passed before I needed the toilet. Unimpressed with my lack of visions, I walked the barren corridor, which continued to extend with time. My brain became more like spaghetti with every step. I didn't know where I was or why I was even there. It stuck me I might be stuck in a haunted hotel with dead people wanting to feed on my soul. No, I was lost in that coffee shop, lost in debt, lost in not knowing what I should do with my life or why I was even born in the first place.

My friend finally found me unable to move in front of the bathroom door with a sign that read 'out of order'.. We wandered back, forgetting our coffees, and ventured into the icy winter night in Philadelphia far from our family homes in Texas. I always hated the cold. It never felt right.

I was hoping to find her again, find definite answers. It was my thinking we would have better luck taking hallucinogenic drugs than using some shit eBay Ouija board. Hector could have told me we were climbing Everest without oxygen. I was ready. "Tell me when."

Hector contacted his cousin, Manolo, in Catemaco, who was also a curandero from a long line of male curanderos, for any advice on enhancing the experience with the drug and to bless the house. He was the one who sourced them for Hector. Manolo refused to enter the US for fear of never returning, or worse. He'd heard the stories about the border and was terrified. There was evil at work and he wanted no part of it. We decided to ask Pastor Rich to keep an eye on us. This would be a bootleg, shoestring ceremony of enlightenment.

★   ★   ★

The old man sat in the pew, switching from scribbling down ideas for his next sermon to rubbing his chest, which was nothing but fire these days. Not a single thought came to mind that he felt passionate about. Not that it mattered. Year after year his congregation was whittled down as people flocked to the big churches on the highway with a full band, lights and cameras.

He was a spiritual dinosaur on the eve of the spiritual apocalypse. His brain was tied up thinking about the proof, actual proof there was something else out there. When the spirit, or whatever it was at Hector's house, made an appearance, no one noticed the old man on the stairs watching everything, hearing *that* voice. He couldn't help but feel angry it wasn't a sign from *his* God performing miracles like the ones in the Bible during a time in history that needed a miracle or two to get mankind to survive longer than another century. He cursed his doubt. But wasn't that where faith was supposed to come in? At that moment he had no desire to believe in something else that might not be of God, or pure. It killed that boy, after all. It took Tanya's heart.

Then his thoughts shifted to Janice, that doomed infatuation that could have been love. Finding out she was pregnant at the time of her death, and that she had been involved in the murder, closed him off forever. His innocence was lost the day he saw Milagros on the tree. He never trusted himself with love again, only the love he felt for God, and now that was being taken away. He put the pad and pencil down and closed his eyes. Before a prayer could escape his lips, the click of the storage room door could be heard.

It slowly opened.

Two shiny marbles reflecting the light from the large windows in the main vestibule stared at him. His soul was ready and so was his body. Most of the people he knew and loved were dead or in ill health. He was beginning to feel like the only one left alive and only half alive at that. Lately he felt weak, sick. But he could still get to his feet unaided. He stood to face the eyes.

"You can't have my soul, demon."

A deep laugh like notes from a cello escaped the room. "I know your soul cannot be mine. It belongs to your God. He is such a jealous God and one even I do not want to cross. This is his realm, for the most part. Besides, I have already fed on another."

Pastor Rich stepped forward to show his defiance. "I know. Tanya. She's dead."

"Yes. And please don't call me a demon. I am nothing of the sort because such things do not exist in *my* world. I'm a visitor from a place beyond where this universe ends and another begins. I am one that fills the voids of your imagination. I'm neither evil nor good, kind or hateful. I just am."

"What do you want from me? I'm not scared of you." He waited for her to show herself, but the Queen remained in the dark.

"I want you to be Hector and Belinda's guide. Give them spiritual guidance, just as you have with so many others in your long life. You need not fear me. You were good to Milagros and the people of the field by learning their language and offering aid when you could over the years. I have no quarrel with you."

"Please don't harm anyone else. It's wrong."

The thing in the closet let out a screeching hiss. "Don't preach to me about wrong, not on this soil. The soil of this continent is a mound of congealed blood and shredded, whipped flesh that is tilled century after century with an iron rake of hate. And the churches of the word. What chaos they have made!"

He was too old and had seen too much to argue with that. "I'll do my best for Belinda and Hector because they're good people. Not my place to judge. I serve only one God." Pastor Rich didn't trust the thing, but he found no reason to go against its wishes.

"Thank you. Don't worry, old man, you will see your God soon enough. Would you like me to show you?"

The offer was tempting, to see how he would die. His pulse quickened in a way that scared him at his age. One odd palpitation could be the end.

"No, just let it be. I know it will be soon."

The two lights were gone. Pastor Rich jumped at the sound of the doors behind him opening. Speak of the Devil.

*   *   *

Before we could ask our question with a very rehearsed explanation, Pastor Rich waved us forward. "Go on, I'm listening. My answer is yes, but I still want to hear it."

We gave him the long explanation of our needing a spiritual guide while in a drug-induced state.

"I'll do as you ask, but I have to tell you I don't agree with drugs. We had AA meetings here for a spell. I saw so many boys leave for Vietnam and return a mess from that stuff. Buried a few over the years, too. Not that it was the drugs' fault. That damn war. I won't ever forget the stories told to me right here in this church. No one should see that. No one should experience that, anywhere. My hope is to die before I see any more wars. When do you want to do this?"

We wanted to do it the following day.

*   *   *

We opened the main living room for the first time since the death of the boy. Dust clung to stale air, but nothing felt off about the room. It was so clean – thanks to a hired crew – you would have never known anything had occurred. I was happy Pastor Rich was there because we knew him. We had no idea what would happen.

Hector and I sat facing each other. Pastor Rich sat next to us with his Bible at one side. We brought the dried mushrooms to our lips and chewed, then washed them down with cold water. The journey began as a whirlpool in my mouth, traveling to my stomach. I thought of the time I gave my first blow job at nineteen and how the semen crashed against my tongue, slightly choking me as it went down in globs. I was excited and slightly sickened. My empty belly accepted the sludge.

*　　*　　*

As the mushrooms take effect, I'm taken back to my first sleepover at nine and my friend Rosa wants to play house. Wearing only oversized t-shirts before bed, she's the dad and I'm the mom. She shoves her tongue in my mouth and her hand down my panties without warning. I don't know what she's doing or how she knows any of this, but I know I don't like playing house this way. I tell her we should watch a horror film instead. Something shatters in me after that. Is it wrong, or right? I feel confused and shaken. The TV is on and I fall asleep to *Demons*.

My brain is wrapped in warm cloth, the kind they put on your face before a facial or the kind you do at home when the hangover is unbearable. I'm alone in a dark room that soon becomes filled with house music pounding rhythmically against my chest. I can feel the vibrations of sound fighting against my skin until it breaks through to reach my core. There are people I don't know, yet I want to kiss them all. Spinning, dancing, high as a fucking kite on ecstasy, I'm twenty-one, in a club with an escort I work with. Faces are rubbed-out contorted shadows of strobe lighting and their hair is something you would see on the back of a lizard. In these days my switch is always swinging between self-destruct mode and getting by. All these things I have to do to just get by. The dizziness is like the dazzling light I stare at while the doctors cut me open as I wait to see my child. The only emotion is the dread that my life will never be the same again, but I don't know how. I can't see past that moment because there is nothing to adequately prepare you for parenthood in the history of mankind. There is no pain or sound, just that light staring back at me. The light is cut short. I've blacked out after a night out with girlfriends, knowing I have to end things. I grip the handrail of my staircase, falling twice. Instead of standing, I crawl to my bedroom and fall against the door as I tell my then husband I want a divorce.

I don't remember any of this. I only remember what he tells me and a few other little pieces. He doesn't want a woman like me anyway, a bad drunk, someone so restless. Who would? Who in their right mind would ever want me?

I close my eyes, which are already shut. There she is, Mictecacíhuatl, in the middle of a cave with stalactites above her head. It is silent except for the sound of water droplets hitting small pools around our feet. Her entire body is a naked shade of crimson rope looking as soft as velvet. I want her to let me in. Her head is adorned with vibrant green quetzal feathers attached to an embroidered band. She wears a double string of jade stones around her neck, so shiny they almost glow. She takes off her headdress and motions for me. She wants me to come closer and feel Milagros. Clear fluid is draining from between her legs. It is almost time. With her abdominal muscles separated, I can see the child inside of her uterus, which is like a translucent plastic bag. The little pink thing floats in contentment despite the womb contracting, guiding the infant out into the world. Mictecacíhuatl squats in a birthing position in a shallow pool of water and I kneel before her. Between her legs I can see the head of a baby crowning. I don't know what to do, but I know I am the only one who can do it. From the shadows, indigenous women dressed in warriors' armor decorated like the coat of a jaguar emerge and surround my Queen. This armor is usually reserved for men. They steady her arms around their shoulders to make pushing more comfortable. She doesn't scream or cry; only chants, "La Reina de Las Chicharras", over and over until she lets out a moan that sounds more like an orgasm than a shout of childbirth pain.

I pull the bloody baby out with ease and a flutter of chicharras follow. The umbilical cord is a long snake that detaches at the rattle. The creature licks the infant's foot and slithers away singing its rattle song of joy. This baby girl is perfect, with eyes as black as her mother's. I feel like I am not holding a baby, but something from somewhere I can't understand. What is the story that has created this creature? The Queen takes the baby from me and places her on her breast. She looks at me and bows her head. "Milagros is here, and nothing will ever be the same." The shadow handmaidens crowd around her and I am pushed into the dark corner.

★   ★   ★

I opened my eyes. The need to vomit overwhelmed me. Pastor Rich held my hair as the black liquid forced itself from my body. Hector snored with his bucket in his hands and his mouth curled in a small smile. It appeared Pastor Rich had been taking good care of us, because the room wasn't too messy. According to him, neither of us moved once, like statues in a church. It was the scariest experience of his life. I looked at the clock; eight hours had passed since we took the drugs.

I told Pastor Rich to rest in one of the rooms, as I felt well enough to sit and think about what I had experienced. It might not have been real here, but perhaps somewhere else. I didn't want to talk about it just yet. Hector awoke half an hour later and vomited just as violently as I had.. I handed him water and a towel. "You want to talk?"

He finished most of the bottle in one drink, his Adam's apple bobbing up and down in quick succession. "Not much to talk about. I was in this house the entire time, just doing normal things in a home; laundry, cooking, mowing the lawn, which I hate doing and pay someone to do, but I was doing it. I saw kids. I don't know if they were mine or guests. I felt happy, not sad, not that permanent black mood that I usually wake up with. I don't know. It wasn't as clear as the first time I did it and knew without any doubt what I needed to do. It was like I was watching a movie of my life. It was a good life. My grandmother said she would be leaving me again and that I would no longer hear her voice."

CHAPTER TWELVE

"What do you believe, preacher?" Monica Cortez leaned forward in her chair, giving Pastor Rich a soft smile to make him feel like he was talking to an old friend instead of a television journalist.

Pastor Rich wore his best suit and what was left of his hair slicked to the side. He knew he looked old because his aging face was a mask when he looked in the mirror compared to the pile of photos of himself from his youth. The next Billy Graham had been his dream. Now his time was over; he could feel it. After the murder, his ambition faltered and never completely recovered.

"I saw that happen, and I don't know. I've been blessed with a lot of years to serve God and people. But I've also listened to people's hurts – what's been done to them or what they have done. Is this really a plan? Is mysterious really a good thing? Now we've seen something that we can't explain. There are altars cropping up everywhere to this Queen. We are seeing the Virgin Mary and this otherworldly being called upon to do miracles. I really, really do not know what I believe. But I am old and I'll most probably die soon. If I can come back and tell you, I will. I'll know soon enough." He nodded, looking past Monica.

"This is Monica Cortez covering what we are all calling the miracle of La Reina de Las Chicharras."

Pastor Rich felt exhausted by the time the crew cleared out. He dragged his feet to his bedroom to take off his tie and change out of his Sunday dress shoes, which he hadn't worn in three weeks because there had been no services. No flock, no message. His thoughts strayed to Tanya as he sat on his bed, hands and back aching as he pulled off the shoes. The pressure from bending over brought on a coughing fit. He coughed a lot these days, but wasn't that age? He didn't want to end up in a bed, full of sores. He was sure Belinda and Hector would visit if he asked but he didn't want that. He tried to keep watch on his remaining family in Kansas on Facebook, but it was all too much work, the loneliness. He should have moved back to Kansas years ago to be with his extended family, who he hardly knew.

With the soft slippers on his feet, he went to the fridge for a beer. There was one can of Coors left and not much else. It opened with a spray. He would sit in front of *Jeopardy!* not watching but liking the sound of different voices. Made the house feel less quiet. He sat in the recliner, feeling ready. When the last of his beer was gone, he looked to his left. There she was, but not like he last saw her.

"Milagros?" He squinted. Her hair lay flat against her head. Her white shirt was clean and neatly pressed, and the jeans without stains or tears, held up by a thick leather belt. The boots looked like they were the right size.

"Yes, Rich." She walked closer to him. "Do you know why I am here?"

"Is it time?" He lifted his head towards her like a child.

She nodded.

He began to sob. His chest felt on fire with the overwhelming need to cough as he struggled to catch his breath. All his regret, his heartache, the way it made him feel to see death up close, and then hear death's voice so many years later. But his God, the one he sacrificed it all for, remained silent. There was no time left for anything. The one life he was given was over.

"I'm sorry! I'm so sorry for what they did to you. God, I hope I did enough!" He brought his hands to his face, scared of what came next.

"Shhh. You have nothing to fear." Milagros sat on the armrest of the chair and cradled his head, giving his age-spotted forehead a kiss. "It is a privilege and a gift to go like this, in peace."

He nodded again and wiped the tears with the back of his hand. "I know, I know, and I'm ready. I did the best I could. I tried."

"It is all any of us can do."

"Will you take my heart now?"

"No, your heart belongs to another. You will see it all. I wanted to say goodbye and wish you well on your journey."

He laid his head back against the recliner and closed his eyes to Milagros holding his hand.

The preacher passed away peacefully and was found a day later by the young man he employed to take care of the cleaning of the church and bring him groceries. He had no children or wife and only his small congregation and few remaining friends attended the funeral. He would rest peacefully four plots away from Milagros. Belinda could visit them together, cry for people she didn't really know, but loved anyway.

*　　*　　*

On what felt like the shortest day of the year, I declared at happy hour in a bar to my Philadelphian friends, "Ladies, I am going home."

"But you *are* home. One minute you were just leaving for a wedding, and then you were on TV." My friend Nicole poured me another glass of wine that I pushed away.

I hugged her, knowing I could never explain the toll of not being in a place where all my extended family lived and where my ancestors found their way to. All that time I wasted trying to fit in and be like those I deemed to be more successful than me. There was never any space for me there.

Veronica squealed on the phone when I told her about my relocation because she had just found out she was expecting her first child. "You'll have to give me all your advice! You've done this before." The joy and excitement in her voice made me long to be there sooner and watch her belly grow.

My son accepted a place at a small liberal arts school in a suburb of Philadelphia the following year, which meant neither his father nor I would be needed much. He was my little chicharra ready to find a branch in the world. Our relationship was progressing, with a trip planned to Mexico during his first school break.

I found a job with a nonprofit helping battered women rebuild their lives. If I couldn't find justice, then I could at least help women pick up the pieces of their dreams.

Another aspect of my life I decided to clean up was my relationship with my mother, who had begun to show her age. It scared me. After Pastor Rich's death, I decided to let go of my bitterness towards a woman who did the absolute best she could with the limited resources she had, even living with a man we both knew she never really loved but needed. I went through my teens being called a little bitch and feeling like a kick beneath the dining table was what I deserved. My mind didn't want to forgive or forget. I chose to forgive because carrying the pain of feeling unlovable was a burden that was burying me for half my life, and I didn't even realize it. Mothers suffer just as much as their children. I took the time to call her, ask about her life, but mostly let her know that I did love her, even those times I cursed her out so that my pain could be felt like a belt against her heart. I spit as much hurtful venom as I could scour from the pit of my damaged insides. With that wound healing slowly, I felt truly fulfilled without a man filling a space next to me.

After much deliberation, I said yes to being Hector's surrogate. The egg came from a young twenty-something Chicana studying in San Antonio and the sperm from Hector.

I was just a vessel.

Hector and I lived a good, harmonious life together. During my free time I assisted with the farm business. I was sure we would move on with other people at some point, but being together without being together romantically was a relaxed comfort.

Benny and Hector visited each other regularly, splitting their time between Mexico and Texas. I didn't pry, but I hoped it was the start of something special for them both. Hector was reluctant and scared to pursue anything serious with their lives in different countries and his desire to start a family. However, it was only a matter of time before they would become a family. I could feel that. As you can imagine, when the supernatural had been documented at the farmhouse, Hector received call after call for private tours and from people wanting to stay the night. Some offered ridiculous money. We regularly performed limpias to spiritually cleanse the house and also set up an altar dedicated to his family. Benny sent us the photo of Concepcion and Milagros when they were young for the altar. Also on the altar was a photo of Pastor Rich that we'd been given at his funeral.

Hector awoke one morning and declared, "It's time to open up business again. My father left me a message in my dream. I can't be afraid. I need to claim my power as a curandero and a businessman." Within a week he'd booked the farm for a solid eight months. This required Hector to hire a full-time assistant, groundskeeper and housekeeping staff. He opened for fully vetted individuals who believed. *She* spoke to him, telling him who to allow in. Hector embraced his brujo blood and spent long hours in meditation, listening to the voices he never wanted to hear before. Like me, he'd searched in vain for fulfillment and validation out *there*. A degree on a sheet of white paper cannot change preconceived notions about your brown skin.

We found our own place. The farm is a sort of mecca for those looking for answers they haven't found elsewhere. There are rows of benches surrounding the ceiba tree in a concentric circle. Ten feet around the tree there are offerings of prayers that people leave for themselves or loved ones. Tokens of remembrance for the life Milagros lived so she might never be forgotten. Newspaper clippings of things that worry people, prayer cards, anything that anyone wanted to lay at the feet of a deity who could be seen and heard, which made us feel the same. Globally, the Queen of the Dead is now as revered as La Virgen. Organized religions are not happy about it, but there is nothing they can do about it. They no longer control the narrative. A cult of nasty women, as some called it.

Hector allowed a team from the Vatican to stay in the house and observe. With nothing supernatural occurring, they stated the phenomenon was nothing except simple idolatry, a way of accepting things that are unacceptable and blasphemous. It was one big hoax to instill anarchy when order was needed. I looked at my own life, those who passed from here, and those caged, or those floundering behind an internal and external border. Sometimes blasphemy can be the impetus for necessary change.

Just when life cradled me in routine, a coin was flipped, and fate presented me with a door.

★   ★   ★

Pastor Rich's church sat empty for months. The tiny congregation tried to find someone to fill the pastor position, but no one wanted it. Eventually the congregation was absorbed into the megachurches with the live bands and cameras. Their signs tower on the highway, always giving clear directions where to find them. The church, which was as old as Hector's home, would be left to rot as a relic of a time passed until it was bought by a tech and robotics businessman from Mexico intent on taking humans to space.

★   ★   ★

Arie Fernandez showed up on a bike in head-to-toe cycling gear that made him look like he had just finished the Tour de France. A semi-retired billionaire, he spent his time exploring interests other than counting money. There was nothing pretentious or crass about him. It must have been his humble roots. His grandmother, Rebecca Shure, was a Jewish immigrant from Europe who fled to Mexico when they were denied safe haven in the United States as the rise of fascism threatened to exterminate their family. They escaped with their lives and very little else. Mexico was a safe option for sanctuary after landing in Cuba, where they were not really welcomed. Once settled in Mexico, she met a rancher. Together they built a business and a family that prospered. Arie started his venture capital business from the ground up, and with solid investments in tech throughout the years, he was on the cover of every business and news magazine as the genius who would change the world.

When I opened the door, I knew I was in trouble. A man at least six foot three with a solid body that could be clearly seen through his cycling gear stood on the front porch with a bike, the type you see professional cyclists use. The fitted Lycra top unzipped to the center of his chest showed enough muscle and hair to make me want to reach out and grab him by the waistband of his shorts, which were just as tight as his top. I couldn't tell if his sea-colored eyes were blue or green against skin as brown as mine. Our nature never changes, and my lust would never be tamed. What made me think celibacy would ever be a viable option?

"It's Belinda, right?"

I knew who he was, but I didn't know why he was here.

"Hi. That's me, can I help you?"

"I'm Arie." He wiped the sweat off his hand on a towel tied to the handlebars of his bike before extending it to me. "I wanted to introduce myself because I just purchased the church. I'd love to talk to you about it. My plan is to dedicate it to Mictecacíhuatl when it's refurbished."

Hector was in Mexico introducing Benny to his family and my son had just left from a weekend here. I had the house all to myself, which was very bad because once Arie shook my hand, my thoughts were only of having him all over and inside my body. I cursed myself. He could be married or unavailable, or not interested in women. I took his hand so as not to appear rude.

"Come in. How about iced tea? You look...hot." I immediately realized I was betraying my desire.

"Iced tea sounds great." His hand still held mine as his eyes brightened. He laughed lightly when he answered, which told me he saw the discourse in my mind playing out on my face. The attraction was mutual. I knew that look, could feel the chemistry. The dampness of his skin made me think of the climate between my legs. I wanted my sheets to stink with our mingling saliva and lubrication. I'd happily roll over on the wet spot on the bed when we were finished. That is when you know you really love or want someone; you don't give a fuck about the wet spot.

We talked through a few glasses of iced tea. Pleasantries mostly, before I prepared us a simple lunch of Parma ham, French mustard and melted cheese sandwiches. To my surprise, someone had moved the hands of the clocks to early evening.

"Have you been to the tree yet?" I asked while fighting the urge to wipe crumbs from his mouth. We weren't at that point yet, and I told myself it was only the crumbs and not his lips that held my attention.

"I have, and it's a place that should be preserved. It's one of the reasons I bought the church. The plaque is beautiful."

I didn't want to appear overeager, so I didn't tell him it was my creation. "If you have time, we can go there now?"

"I'd love to. But I have to say you have a bit of mustard there. I've been staring for a while now. I wanted to tell you before we go out." His hand brushed against the corner of my mouth and cheek, lingering. I was in trouble. He was in trouble. It was only due to my promise to myself to be less hasty that I didn't maul him on the spot.

"Thanks, but so do you. Right here." I stood before him with the bottom of my breasts at about mouth height. I would have paid good money to feel him wrap his hands around my hips and pull me close, his fingers sliding down to squeeze the bottom of my ass where it met my thighs. I wanted my fingers in his thick black wavy hair while his mouth explored my breasts, my erect nipples scraping against his stubble. Then he could soothe them with his tongue and mouth.

Instead I brushed away the crumbs, and crumbs that didn't even exist, on the other side of his mouth. I wanted to touch him.

"White wine?" I stepped back to regain my composure before I did something impulsive, because impulse control was a problem most of my life.

"I like it all. And I'll try anything."

Before either of us made a move, I stepped away to grab a bottle of wine from the fridge and a blanket from the storage bench in front of the kitchen window. We walked to the tree with only a few visitors that day. The path was no longer brown weeds, but a pebbled walkway lined with crosses, photos and idols of the La Virgen and Mictecacíhuatl.

It's not okay to straddle and make out with someone you met hours before in front of strangers, so I kept my hands to myself but let my eyes tell him I was available if he wanted me.

We chose a bench away from the others, who wandered around. The conversation, recounting our lives, poured as easy as the Chenin Blanc we drank over the next few hours. When the crowd thinned after sunset and our wine was finished, I felt comfortable enough to ask him something personal.

"Why did you buy the church, really? Why Mictecacíhuatl?"

He slouched on the bench so that his head rested on the back edge. He looked at the stars, which were bright and clear because of the remoteness of the property, the darkness. We kept the lights to a minimum, using solar Christmas lights strung randomly on benches. The magic here needed to be preserved. His beautiful face and full lips made for kissing were softly illuminated.

"My roots are Jewish and Mexican. Jews don't have a definitive answer for an afterlife. When I saw that video with the Queen peering from the bathroom, her voice, everything I believed was challenged. So, I called on her in a mirror and I saw my death. I was in a hotel room after a bad meal of room service and half a bottle of wine. It was awful. I'm forty-five years old with no children and an aging family. I've lived a life most people dream about but none of it mattered and no one could save me from fate. I'm retired now. I spend my free time cycling, working with charity, investing in projects to save mankind one day, and now this church." That was when he turned to face me. All my self-control was needed not to fuck up this moment and jump him. "She brought me to you."

I know he didn't mean me; he meant this place, but I couldn't shake the feeling those stars were witnessing a story we didn't know we were characters in. We sat looking at each other with nothing else to say. The blanket wasn't big enough to cover us both and I shivered from the freshness of the night, or maybe it was the cold nuclear fusion happening between us. "I should probably go. You think I can get an Uber out here?"

"Not a problem."

He managed to get an Uber quickly as he walked me back to the house that I wished he was staying at. We were not taking guests when he tried to arrange accommodation at the farmhouse. The receptionist didn't recognize his name and I blessed her for that because I wanted him more than ever. But I knew I needed more time to heal my emotional wounds. To be happy alone.

"I'm leaving tomorrow night, but I would like it very much if we could keep in touch. I can't remember the last time I sat and spoke to someone like this. My girlfriend – soon to be ex – and I haven't really spoken in a while. Relationships can be lonely places. But can I ask a favor?"

"Sure." I was begging the Queen he would ask to kiss me.

"Can I leave my bike here? Just until I'm settled?"

Damn. "Of course. Leave it on the porch and I'll take care of it."

"Thanks. Here's my phone. Why don't you give me your contact information?"

Speechless and aroused, I typed my number then followed him on Instagram. "Sandwiches when you get back?"

He laughed, standing close to me. "It's a date."

I watched him climb into an Uber and leave.

★   ★   ★

Hector returned to the farm tan and glowing like he had spent months on a cruise ship sipping cocktails by a pool. Love looked good on him.

"I'm in love and I want to have that baby," he declared over coffee and gifts he brought back for my son and me.

We began the process of IVF while Arie and I tried to keep the relationship in the friend zone. I stared at his photos with a desire to reach out and touch him. It only led to me pleasuring myself, coming hard, thinking about what it would be like to take him between my legs, that mouth sucking me to climax. I'd finish feeling more frustrated and grumpier than before. *Girlfriend. Soon-to-be-ex*, I grumbled, my insecurities getting the best of me. She was probably half my age with her natural beauty still intact. I shifted my attention back to my real life and not the imagined one in my head. I focused on ridding myself of jealousy and envy. Both as awful as soot on my soul.

Veronica was busy with impending motherhood, work and her marriage. I would go days without my emails or texts being answered, but I understood her distance. I had been there. Once the baby arrived, I would visit, but not expect much from her. Motherhood is a sprint from day one.

CHAPTER THIRTEEN

Hector and IVF. From what I read it would be a long process of false starts, tears, all mixed up with hormones. Besides my son and work, I didn't want any distractions. It was grueling and emotional. Trying to conceive, like wanting something above all else and not getting what you want, is true suffering. He suffered more than me, but seeing the disappointment on his face every time we failed cut me.

Arie inevitably became a distraction from this. His texts, photos and emails. We were electronic pen pals who really wanted to fuck. Arie was like me; relationships did not come easy for him. Work had prevented him from putting down roots in any one place long enough to focus on one person. When every city introduces you to new people, the mind and eye forget the heart is somewhere else. When your soul has been stripped enough times, it becomes as restless as a ghost. Ain't no pinning it down. We were both tired of broken promises, so we didn't make any to each other.

Then I received a text I am not ashamed to say I was happy to receive. There was no longer a girlfriend. I couldn't wait for him to return.

We agreed love was exhausting so we were content with each other's company, hands and lips. I said friend zone, I didn't say no intimacy zone. Everything except sex, like we were in high school. It was the healthiest romantic relationship in my life.

Hector would wink at me when the three of us would bump into each other in the kitchen in the morning. I spared him no details, and he took it all in like a gossip magazine. He knew there was no way I could become pregnant with Arie because I was saving that for our doctor's appointments. Every month I emerged from the bathroom to an expectant Hector only to give him disappointing news. Every month I bled.

It took six months for the church to be refurbished. It was only by Arie's pockets and watchful eye that a stunning sanctuary worthy of pilgrimage and a queen was created. Every Friday there would be a mass of sorts for people to sing and share their stories of heartache and hope, a never-ending festival for the living and the dead to be as one. There were no barriers to who could attend as long as they had an accepting heart. Mictecacíhuatl did say she wanted everyone.

The night before the church would be unveiled to the public, Arie invited me to be the first to see it. We went at eleven p.m., when most of the visitors had gone. The bones of the exterior remained the same, except all the broken pieces were replaced and there was a new roof. A coat of fresh white paint made the walls glow. The simplicity felt welcoming. I had to catch my breath when I walked through the door. It was better than all the megachurches, and even though it was not nearly the same size, I had the same awe as I did for the cathedrals in Europe, created for the same reason as this one: to inspire. All my senses prickled and felt stimulated at once. The wood that was chipped and rotting away was completely restored to a golden amber varnish that felt like fire in the candlelight. Pale lighting encased in colorful glass orbs blown in Mexico hung from the rafters like planets. Murals of saints painted by Mexican artists decorated the walls. Dried herbs filled the entire place with a sweet, earthy scent. In the front was an altar with fresh flowers and candles. On the floor lay soft bedding similar to a futon. He knew me well enough to bring a basket filled with food and wine. From his phone he controlled music that played from speakers mounted on the walls.

I didn't want to eat or drink unless it was his flesh or fluids. We had been in this unspoken tug of war and flirtation that left me in knots night after night. Between the stolen lunches, dinners and texts, I simply couldn't wait any longer. The fooling around wasn't enough. Hector and I were taking a break from IVF. It didn't look like anything would happen and we agreed he should find someone younger.

All my life I'd been favoring instant gratification. This was the longest I had waited for anyone. Tonight, there would be nothing left of each other. I needed him to devour every inch of me. It would be here, in *her* house, under the light of the glass and the warmth of a rededicated church. As he opened the wine, I placed one hand on his hip, grabbed the bottle, and placed it on the altar. His large hands pulled me close; the firmness of his erection against my body caused my growing excitement to ache. For months I had been choking on my arousal, opting to pleasure myself with his photos instead of scrolling through bad late-night porn on my phone.

He was easily twice my size, with solid brown skin like my own. Hair covered most of his chest. There was no escaping his flesh as his cock crushed me closer to orgasm with every thrust after all this time. The rhythm of our fucking kept time with music by Maluma playing on a loop. We had all night, which was just enough time to carry out half the fantasies that I used in my bed when I needed to get off and yet still felt frustrated despite experiencing every other sexual act with him. The reality was infinitely more pleasurable than the fantasy. Most of my existence was fantasy anyway. Every part of him tasted more delectable with him locked inside of me. Our bodies moved with ease as the sweat lubricated our skin in celebration of the Queen who had brought us together. Just like he said the first night we met.

On my hands and knees as he glided in and out of me from behind, I looked to the mural of Mictecacíhuatl, remembering how much she excited me. I felt dizzy with pleasure and pain, with his cock becoming more engorged as he neared climaxing. In that moment I sensed she was with us. The candles dimmed suddenly. My flesh prickled. He pulled out and flipped me to my back.

With my legs resting against his chest as he pumped inside of me, Mictecacíhuatl made her presence known. She hovered behind Arie. Her face floated just above his right shoulder. While one of her hands traced his bicep and forearm, the other ran down my leg, causing me to shudder. The overwhelming need to orgasm from her touch and his cock stroking me made me feel as if I couldn't breathe. My desire for both of them strangled me in ecstasy. If only the three of us could be stripped of our flesh and intertwine ourselves into one. Intimacy on a cellular level in a body that was as temporary as a condom. My hand moved to between my legs as I watched him and the Queen. Her black eyes beckoned me to allow her to pull me through to another place we cannot feel or see. His jade eyes widened when her hand moved between his legs to gently massage his testicles. Never have I experienced that degree of excitement as I submitted to pleasure. The fated love between us sparked and bloomed in the center of my clit and scattered across the nerves in my thighs until it reached my throat. I cried out from the fallout. I couldn't help myself.

If nirvana existed, I had found it. My orgasm didn't want to end. Instead I continued to buck my hips harder, stimulating my clit with my fingers as I exploded again, looking at my beautiful Arie. He cried out with the Queen still behind him. Her tongue licked his ear followed by a kiss on his neck, which bulged with veins. Then she was gone. Six months I had waited for him and that sexual encounter. It was worth the wait. Arie would remain in my bed from that moment on.

★   ★   ★

The New Church of Mictecacíhuatl opened to the public on a Saturday to a crowd that couldn't be fully accommodated by the small town. It was a global event that attracted more people by the day. Hector worried about the protesters even though Arie hired private security. Just as people wanted to be part of something never experienced in their lifetime, there were those who wanted to see this new way of thinking destroyed. They were vicious trolls attached to their hate because that was their identity. That was until Milagros herself, La Reina de Las Chicharras, chased them off.

Clashes occurred more frequently as the political heat was turned up to match the heatwave that was occurring globally. The protesters showed up one night during an impromptu live performance by a popular band that didn't announce they would be there. It reminded me of Nirvana doing their iconic MTV acoustic set. Some scumbag shouting insults threw a flaming bag of shit into the peaceful crowd doing their best to ignore the bigots and just focus on the music. Before the bag could harm anyone, Milagros, La Reina de Las Chicharras, appeared. A loud gasp escaped the crowd followed by phones lighting up. She caught the bag, extinguishing the flames upon impact with her hand. The ones who were seated cleared a space around her. She ignored them. Her bruised face with only one eye open stared at the protesters. The sores around her neck from the rope leaked blood that covered her white shirt and dungarees. She looked just as she did upon her death in 1952. Her mouth opened, unhinging her jaw.

"This is what your words look like. This is the form it takes and now you will have to face it! Milagros, La Reina de Las Chicharras!"

She walked towards the people previously spewing hate with

her big boots thudding hard against the ground. Insects chirped wildly. The protesters screamed as they ran to their vehicles, dropping signs and guns. With all the power of Sodom and Gomorrah, she shrieked, calling out a black cloud of wasps from their nests that coated her body like badges. The nests opened like gills on a fish, releasing the little venomous occupants. The creatures had their targets in sight and did not leave until the protesters were injected with their venom.

Milagros turned to face the crowd behind her. Some people covered their eyes, afraid of what they had just witnessed. But she appeared as she did before leaving Mexico. Her expression was that of a saint you see in paintings and a faint glow ringed her body. Then she was gone. It was all caught on video. No one dared to return to the church or the ceiba tree to pick a fight.

CHAPTER FOURTEEN

Hector and Benny wanted to start the IVF journey again, together. I'd already begun to spot, with my womb painfully cramping and my period due. I told Hector to continue to look for younger surrogates who might bring him closer to his dream of a family. As I waited for my period to start, I found the smallest cicada shell left on my dresser next to my bottle of folic acid. Two bloody fingerprints were on each side of the insect's head. Even before I touched the delicate thing, I could feel the vibrations coming from it. There was something inside. I flipped the casing over, careful not to crush a single part of the body. Within the shell there was a soft object that resembled a string, but upon closer inspection, it throbbed. I could feel her. Not Milagros; the other. I didn't know what to do with it except keep it safe. Without pause or thought, I took the small body and placed it in my mouth. As I swallowed, I envisioned the red string threading into my own flesh and becoming one with me. Maybe it would take over. I am just a vessel.

Another unexpected turn by fate or a goddess.

★   ★   ★

The four of us cracked open the second bottle of wine with the roast chicken Arie prepared for dinner. It was a relaxed evening of sharing stories and breaking bread. Benny had just told some joke when my head began to spin. I had felt like that before but not with that small amount of wine.

"Excuse me."

I stood to use the toilet when the smell of the roasted meat curdled in my nose and stomach. The churning food moved quickly up my pipes until I vomited on the floor next to the table.

"Belinda, are you okay?" Arie grabbed napkins for me, with Benny and Hector looking on.

I knew what this was. "Hector, we should see the doctor."

Benny ran out the door with Hector to the Rite-Aid, which was still open. They returned with a plastic bag filled with tests. Benny, the doctor, reassured me it could be anything.

I sat on the toilet, unable to pee the one time I needed to. I squeezed my eyes and my pelvis until I peed enough to saturate the stick. I waited three minutes then looked. I smiled, happy for Hector. I could give him this gift, until I realized Arie and I were having non-stop sex like foolish teens, not always using protection.

I pensively walked out of the bathroom with the stick in my hands. Hector knew me well enough to know the answer. His eyes grew large as he touched my shoulders gently.

"Please tell me...."

I nodded. Before I could say any more, he and Benny embraced, grabbing each other's faces for a deep, passionate kiss before burying their heads in the crook of each other's necks.

"I love you," said Hector in a muffled voice against Benny's shoulder.

"I fucking love you," Benny replied.

I kept silent while they enjoyed the moment. Then I looked to Arie, who I could clearly tell was happy for the men, but wondered what further tests might reveal.

★ ★ ★

Before long I was miserable and couldn't keep food or water down for more than a few hours. Standing for too long caused me to sway like a drunkard even though I had been sober since the test showed positive. The years made me forget how physically challenging pregnancy could be at times. Benny urged me to take a Harmony Test, which would give me information about the baby before the usual twelve-week scan. The wait for the results was excruciating for both Hector and me. Arie did his best to support me as if I carried his child.

When I was finally called back to see the doctor, I was told we needed a scan first. There it was. Black and white, blipping and swishing quickly like the flapping of hummingbird wings. Two sacs, two babies. Hector and I were startled. We'd only implanted one embryo. The chances of it splitting were low.

The doctor continued to prod my belly and take measurements. "Is everything all right?" He looked at me more startled than when we first saw two embryos. "Please excuse me." He rushed out of the room and returned moments later with another doctor, a woman about my age, dressed in fashionable clothing and shoes.

My doctor didn't like the idea of making a mistake, judging by the way he kept his brow furrowed. "Check both. I swear they're at different stages of development. One is older than the other. It's impossible."

The other doctor gave me warm smile and patted my hand. "Just so you know, both are perfectly healthy. I'll double check what my colleague has found."

More painful prodding with the wand. Measuring on the screen. Both doctors slowly looked at Hector and me.

The female doctor spoke again. "Like I said, healthy. But the dating is not very accurate right now. We will check in a few weeks. You may leave now."

It had to be Arie's child. I knew it in my heart. My body felt it.

Hector smiled and said, "Sisters," with tears in his eyes. We agreed to wait further into the second trimester to tell our families the good news. Every scan showed the same thing. One baby was older than the other. But I needed to know. I decided on an amniocentesis. This procedure carried a risk, but I could extract DNA and know for certain. Hector agreed to me doing this; he wanted to know as much as I did. I would only inform Arie when the result came back and if Arie had no interest in the child, Hector wanted to take on the role of father for both children. For him, it was the miracle of a lifetime. Hector's heart astounded me sometimes. He was a true brother to me.

Two sacs, two little girls, two fathers, three mothers.

★ ★ ★

The church was closed for the evening when we walked there after dark hand in hand. It was time to tell Arie the results of the tests he wasn't aware I'd taken. I told Arie I wanted to pray and recreate the first time we were together. My sickness was passing, and my hormones craved sex, but I thought it would be fitting to tell him I carried his child where our daughter was conceived. I know the Queen had this in her cosmic plans. Why else would she have been there? After he pulled out our bedding from the storage room, I made him sit next to me in the first pew. I gave him the news as plainly as I could.

"Wait. You're pregnant with two babies and one is mine. The other is Hector's?"

I felt shame again. I always placed too much concern on what men thought of me, something I hoped my daughter would not do. He didn't need to stick around if he didn't want to. I had a plan. I had thought I needed enough men in my lifetime to know I never really needed them.

"Yes. Here are the results. If you want nothing to do with us, Hector said—"

Before I could say anything else, he slipped his hand beneath my loose blouse. His palm covered my small belly.

"I want you *and* her." He kissed me, making me forget that this was good right now, but a baby is the definition of hard work. Would this last through sleepless nights and temper tantrums? Could we thrive as a couple when I felt betrayed by my body when it had to work overtime to accommodate three lives? I dismissed these thoughts that didn't matter in a moment that felt good, as good as his fingers moving from my belly to between my legs. We slept in the church that night. I stared at the mural of the Queen. I hoped she would appear to me, but I knew there was nothing hidden from her.

★   ★   ★

One of the little girls growing inside of me decided to wedge her head between my pelvic bones, which felt as if they were being ground to dust with every step. Raised bumps covered my body as a reaction to the baby. PUPS occurs in pregnancy when the immune system thinks a foreign body is attacking. The steroids helped, but the itching would not stop until the babies were out. And none of this is said lightly, because I know how hard it can be to conceive. The only thing I wanted besides finally giving birth in Catemaco, Mexico was an extended vacation in the sun with my son and Arie. They would meet for the first time.

My son didn't seem fazed by my pregnancy, or the news he would be a big brother on the cusp of manhood. He was far too concerned with his new car and the class load. I was content with hearing, "I love you, Mom," when we ended our conversations. I remember being that age, and very little concerned me except myself. We planned to rent a home in the Yucatan. Hector's entire family would attend the birth, which would take place at a hospital because of my previous c-section and the fact that I was carrying two babies.

For any woman, as pregnancy progresses, sleep becomes difficult. You can only sleep on your side; they say the left side is best. With less room for the baby to move, every kick and stretch pushes your uterine wall to bursting point. One night their kicks proved too much for my body.

I continued to dream about drowning in the ocean or tumbling down from the top of the pyramid. I was afraid. I was afraid of raising a child, a girl. Just before sunrise I lifted myself out of bed for water. The pain when my feet touched the ground caused me to scream out loud. It felt as if my flesh was unzipping, tiny teeth ripping my insides. Something was wrong. It was not time. I used the wall to guide me to where Hector and Benny were sleeping, because Arie was in Mexico on business. He wanted to build us a new home there. Every step pushed sweat from my pores. I had to get to them. The floor beneath my feet was slippery from my blood. This was not like I imagined. This was not like the vision in the ceremony.

"Hector! Benny!" I screamed between sobs.

Benny was a doctor; there had to be something he could do. When I reached their door, Hector was just opening it. He looked at me with half-opened eyes. Then he saw my blood-soaked legs. One hand held my belly while the other was flat against the wall for support.

"Benny! Benny! Hurry!" I wanted to lie on the floor and fall asleep.

Unlike with his great aunt, Benny went into action. I remember Hector laying me on my side on the cool tiled floor. It felt good on my hot skin. In my mind I called out to anything that would listen. For years I didn't want to exist and now I did. My next memory was of the nurse preparing me for general anesthetic and my arm extended for a blood transfusion. The doctor was between my legs.

"Her uterus has ruptured from her previous cesarean. This is the only way. We need to remove her uterus." See, scars never heal.

I remember nothing of the birth. All was black. Not even the Queen made an appearance.

My next memory was Hector next to me with a small bundle in his arms. He was glowing, despite probably not sleeping since I made my way to his bedroom door.

"How are you?" he asked softy.

I gave him a smile. "Ready for a damn drink on the beach. I'm alive. But the babies, please tell me they're okay."

"Thank La Virgen, Jesus and the Queen, you're all fine. Your daughter with Arie is in an incubator, her lungs were not as developed, but the doctors said she'll be strong enough to breathe on her own in no time. Arie hasn't left her side. Also, it's all over the news."

The pain subsided once I knew my babies were all right. Arie would do anything for the daughter he couldn't wait to meet, even rushing the home he was building for us as a first birthday present she wouldn't remember.

"Why are people interested? This isn't exactly a virgin birth."

"People are curious. The gay curandero, the Mexican Jewish billionaire leading a church dedicated to Mictecacíhuatl, the woman who's given birth to two babies from different fathers? That and they all live in a haunted house? What's not interesting?"

I tried to laugh but the pain only caused a grimace.

"May I have a look?" Hector placed the infant in my arms. She was beautiful, perfect with two large strawberry birthmarks at her temples just above her eyebrows. They looked like hot fingertips had scalded her skin when they placed a crown upon her head. The rest was like all newborns. It would be some time before her features would fill out and we could see the color of her eyes. Her little mouth began to search for my breasts, which were leaking as I held her close. She could smell the milk.

"Will you feed her?"

When I heard these words I instinctively looked around, expecting to see the Queen. It was Hector. I was hesitant because I didn't enjoy breastfeeding. In fact I only breastfed my son for four weeks because I couldn't endure the pain or constant bouts of mastitis. Truth be told, I wanted my life back after his birth. But I knew the importance of at least trying, even if it didn't work out. I placed her little mouth on my nipple, remembering as much as I could about placement. The initial latch feels like a piercing, then it subsides. She was a hungry little girl taking her fill from me. The sweet scent of her head filled me with guilt over all the wasted time not cherishing the little things. I wished I could take all that sand and put it back into the hourglass. But I did the best I could, and I knew my son loved me. This baby was not mine; she was something else. I kissed one of her birthmarks. The infant opened her eyes. I was scared and enamored at the intensity radiating from them.

Hector must have sensed my thoughts. "Do you feel that? She's magic. My sister was the first to bring it to my attention. She held her after the birth. She says we have to keep her safe, loved. She will be home-schooled for the first few years."

I remembered the cicada shell I ate before I knew I was pregnant. "Hector, I need to tell you something. I found a shell with something inside of it. I ate it, but this was before I knew I was pregnant. If anything happens...."

"I know, Belinda. She gave it to me. It was meant to be. I'll have more children, too. Don't worry, you don't have to go through this again for me. I'm sorry. I didn't know the birth would be like this."

I switched the baby to the other breast. The pained expression on his face told me he was truly sorry that the doctors had to remove my uterus. This didn't bother me.

"I didn't plan on having more children."

"I know. But I feel terrible." We shifted our attention from each other to look at the real star in the room.

"What's her name?" I asked as I handed the infant back to Hector now that she was sound asleep and no longer feeding.

"This very special princess, one day a queen, is called Milagros Ix Chel Dominguez."

It was a name fit for a queen. Hector placed the baby in a wheeled bassinet. Hector had chosen a beautiful name. "I also need to let you know your son wants to talk to you. He seems very upset over something. It's an urgent matter he said he won't even discuss with his father. I told him as soon as you were awake and not on the good drugs, you'll contact him."

The last time I spoke to my son, I was fine and we were talking about the things we would see and do on our vacation. Now I was in the hospital post-surgery. Hector handed me my handbag and left to give me privacy. He would be back when baby Milagros was ready to feed.

My son answered my call immediately, which never happened, as if he needed time to think about if he really wanted to speak to me.

"Mom. You okay? I need to tell you something." His voice was shaking. He didn't sound like a young man, but a small child afraid to tell me he had ground Play-Doh into the rug or spilled a pot of paint. There was fear in his voice. "It was supposed to just be a joke."

I knew immediately what he had done, but I needed to hear it from him. I had to believe she wouldn't harm my child.

"I was at Cameron's house. We had a few beers. Sorry. Then we called her. Nobody believed it."

I was asking God in my mind to make everything okay. It was going to be okay. It was a chant that continued even when I spoke. "And?"

His voice was still shaking. "Nothing. They all laughed at me. But last night I had a dream. I saw you die having a baby. Then I had another dream that was like a movie. I've been up all night writing it down. It's called 'The Book of Ikal'. I've emailed you. I don't know what it is, but I had to write it down."

"I love you, baby. I'll read it now. And I'm not angry about the beer as long as you don't drive or anyone else who's been drinking is driving you."

"How are you, Mom? Hector said you had the babies, but you needed surgery."

"I'm going to be okay. I didn't die. You want me to buy you a ticket? We can start that vacation now if you want."

"It's fine. Get better. I'll see you in a few months. Just read that dream. I swear it came out of me like a gospel."

CHAPTER FIFTEEN

The Book of Ikal according to Jacob

All the bodies. All that blood. What did they do wrong to receive such hate from the gods, or were these men gods manifested on earth, as some said? No, he knew these invaders were men. Their lusts were those of men. Ikal knew he was dying. It was just the beginning, but the small red marks on his body told him it wouldn't be long. He had seen so many of his people fall from this plague brought by the pale demons. He would need to use whatever was left of his life to save his daughter, Ix Chel. She had the heart of a warrior in a female body, like a goddess. Her body was a vessel for life and magic. Her body would be the vessel to keep their bloodline safe.

He moved quickly through the thick foliage of the forest and sweat stung his eyes. It was a day past when he needed to bring her fresh supplies. She hid in a hidden hut dedicated to his queen, Mictecacíhuatl. It was a place where he poured as much blood from their enemies as possible and offered their split hearts to show his devotion. He had been hiding Ix Chel for weeks to keep her free from the ropes and eyes of the invaders as well as the sickness. As long as his people continued to fall ill, the invaders wanted more human chattel to refresh their stocks of slaves. Ikal was once a powerful priest with the king, but since that king tried to make a deal with the demons, Ikal had been hiding or fighting. He wouldn't remain long on this earth knowing he was plagued with a sickness no one recovered from.

The small hut looked undisturbed and quiet. His tensed muscles relaxed. He knew she remained safe. Once inside, his heart slowed to its usual steady beat.

"My love, Ix Chel, are you here?"

Ix Chel poked her head from behind the wooden altar. She smiled at her father then rose from the ground. He held a flat palm towards her not to come closer. She sunk inside, knowing she could never hold him again. For the rest of her days she would carry an obsidian knife should she need to take her own life or that of another. Before her brothers were murdered, she had been shown how to use the blade usually meant for warriors.

Before he could speak, he heard a rustle outside the hut. The door burst open. It was one of them. The part of him that had sunk like a sacrifice in a cenote now clenched.

"I knew you were hiding something, you dirty old man. Not only do you sacrifice to Satan, but you have a concubine for him. Not for long. And what is this blasphemy? You'll pay for your worship of that whore god."

Ikal had seen that look in many men's eyes, but not like these demons. Their sport was beyond evil. And his queen was not a whore. She embodied beautiful death, powerful and all that makes the end something to embrace because it is inevitable. The soldier stepped closer.

"Give the girl to me and I might let you live. By the looks of it you don't have much time."

The soldier raised his gun and fired at the bloody stone idol of the queen in the center of the altar. When he saw this blasphemy, Ikal's anger, which began as a silent cry in his mind, traveled to his mouth. The veins in his face, neck and arms protruded as he screamed his queen's name out loud. The soldier feared the sweating, pustule-riddled man intended to kill him. As Ikal rushed to the soldier, a bullet flew into his chest, knocking him down.

He lay there, only sorry he could not have taken the soldier with him into death. Ix Chel would find a way. With his dying breath he told his queen and his daughter he loved them.

Ix Chel had shuffled to the corner of the hut, unable to weep because there had been nothing but tears and sorrow since these things arrived on their shores. The anger that she saw in her father's attack fled his body and jumped into her. Fury and revenge stirred in her blood and it was as delicious as Xocolatl.

The soldier licked his lips with a sneer on his face. "Come with me, girl."

He was already laying down his harquebus and untying the leather around his waist when Ix Chel approached him calmly. Her black eyes sucked the light out of the room and focused all her energy on this invader. She parted her lips as if she was about to invite him into her arms.

"Yes, no need to be afraid, young one. You'll be in my home to serve me and my wife and children, but mostly me."

Ix Chel thrust her hand into his sweat-sodden trousers. His stench rolled in her nose as he threw his head back with closed eyes, letting out a moan. He never saw Ix Chel withdraw her obsidian blade or see it swipe across his belly, spilling out his bowels. He stumbled backwards, looking at his wound then at this girl no older than fourteen pulling out his entrails with a grin on her face. The sparse light falling into the hut cast shadows across her face, making her look like a creature from another world. It would be the last image before his death. She was finding pleasure in his slaughter. He continued to walk backwards until he stumbled over her dead father and fell to the ground.

Ix Chel mounted his body and began to chant the way her father showed her. It was a song from her crib that always soothed her. With another swipe and all her body weight to crush the bones of his chest cavity, she clawed out his heart with her bare hands the way she had seen so many times before but had never done herself. Holding another's mortal life force, the heart of an enemy who would see her enslaved or dead, gave her great pleasure. There was power in her fingertips, which trembled as she continued to stare at the heart up close. She placed the bloody mass on the altar then picked up the fallen idol and laid it next to the heart. Ix Chel fell to her knees, cradling her father's head. She prayed to the Queen to keep his soul comfortable and guide her bloodline through the ages of time. She wanted to live. She begged the Queen to give her the power to survive this apocalypse that was befalling their people. Ix Chel removed her father's heart and wrapped it tightly to dry later and grind it to powder. His death, their power, would live on even when foreign soldiers came to take what was not theirs. More were coming every day. Every day their cruelty was more apparent. Her people would all be slaves soon. Not her. Ix Chel gathered everything she could that she would need to survive the jungle for as long as possible.

It was but a girl's dream she could survive without being found. She was captured by one of her own and taken to a mission to do domestic work. After a year at the mission, she decided to become one with the church to keep from having her virginity spoiled without her permission. She said vows to the god named Jesus, who the church said wanted to marry her without consummation. That was good enough. No one had to know she still practiced her own faith in her own way in her mind. No one had to know she was really hiding in plain sight, blending in to avoid being harassed. The mission was a constant reminder of the terror that befell her people, but at least she could live out her days in relative peace.

During this time, she learned the ways of childbirth. She pulled a new race of babies from the bodies of villagers and the invaders. She found it sad that she would not carry on her family blood. She hated the invaders even more for that.

And then a young priest about the same age as her arrived at the mission. His eyes matched her own; they were heavy with sorrow and his skin was the same color brown. The vestments he wore were ill fitted. He did not look like he belonged. This young man was like a piece of seaweed uprooted and cast upon a distant shore. They both were. Both were trying to hide in plain sight. Ix Chel was mesmerized, curious. What tribe did he come from? He was as beautiful as a quetzal bird. She tried not to stare, but she ached to touch him, to be touched. To kiss him. To feel like a woman in his bed. She was now a woman of twenty. She had long grown weary of pleasuring herself alone, stifling her orgasm even from the moonlight. It seemed all the pleasures of life were forbidden by the church. Pleasing herself alone became another private thing no one had to know about. With all the pain of her world, she doubted Jesus even noticed at all. She doubted the priest noticed her either.

He did notice. How could he not feel the gaze of the indigenous young woman with tattoos on her face and covered head to toe in the garments of a sister? She followed his movements when they encountered each other. At night he whipped himself with knotted rope for thinking of what her naked body might look like under all that cloth. This is what he was told to do. Deny yourself for the glory of *one* God. She must have been a witch to possess his thoughts and dreams the way she did. Many nights he awoke to sticky thighs after fantasizing about her. She would have to leave. He could not have her, therefore he could not be near her. If he heard her voice in his ear, he might go mad.

Ix Chel would have him. This god, this life, this new world order was not worth living without love. She wondered why they punished themselves so. Why would a loving god punish as much as this god did?

That night she wandered to where the priest said his evening vespers. Her heart and stomach somersaulted wildly. She stood behind a column, waiting in the shadows for an opportunity to catch him alone. When he emerged from the chapel to return to his room, she made her presence known and motioned for him to come close. He paused, looking at her if he was trying to work out if this was real or a waking dream. From the little light that illuminated the mission at this hour, she could see there was torment on his face. He looked around to ensure no one would notice what he was about to do. When they came face to face, the closest they had ever been, her hand found his hand.

"Come with me. I want you to be with me now."

He knew he must be mad because he would do as she commanded. Under the cover of darkness, she led him to a place away from the mission.

He could feel himself shivering at her touch. Her power was intoxicating. There was no fighting the sensation or his desire. He felt like Adam being led by Eve to eat of the fruit. He now knew how a man could betray everything.

Ix Chel led him to a secluded spot, one that she had known. They didn't need to speak, because when they came to a stop their bodies embraced, needed to be close. She kissed with all the passion left untapped all these years. All the yearning to be touched concentrated in her tongue, which slipped into his mouth. They both began to remove their garments, the foreign horrible things that protected them from the hell they were taught to fear. This moment they shared felt like the heaven their hearts needed. The young priest wanted to weep upon feeling her warmth against his. Her soft flesh was better than anything he had imagined. She led him to the ground and guided him inside of her body.

The first time didn't last long, but the vitality of youth kept them on the floor of the jungle until the early light of the sun could be seen. She looked at his body, his dark flesh and those eyes that could be from a nightmare but felt like a dream, like his body when he was inside of her.

His cheek rested against her bare breast. "What is your name?"

"Ix Chel, but the church has renamed me Isabella. Like a queen. And you?"

"Santiago. What did we just do?"

"Come to me." He followed her instruction as he did before. Ix Chel kissed his perfect mouth. "We did what our bodies were meant to do. Love each other. It is natural. We both wanted it. This place is not meant for us."

He didn't feel like he had committed a sin; he felt like he had been set free. They returned to the mission before anyone could see them. Both knew their fate had changed.

They met as often as they could at the spot in the jungle near a grand ceiba tree with vines so long, they created a curtain they could lie behind.

One night Santiago knew something was wrong when they promised to meet, yet he found she was not lying naked behind the vines. She was fully dressed, standing in front of the tree.

"Are you well, my love?"

Ix Chel smiled with tears in her eyes, fearing the worst. She had seen how the new people were. "We are a trinity now."

Santiago knew exactly what she meant. He fell to his knees and placed his face on her abdomen. His little seed was an apple growing inside of her. He stood to meet the eyes of the woman who carried his progeny. There was only one thing to do.

"We leave this place. We become a family. I do not want this life without you or my child."

Ix Chel felt elation. She was so sure he would abandon her or worse. This first sin would lead to another sin. They would have to take from the church to survive out there. Ix Chel had already told one of the village women of her pregnancy and arranged to flee alone. She would go to the woman and arrange for clothing and supplies for the priest.

Together they cast themselves from the mission and the ill-fitting clothing that hid them from the world. They would set out for a place where no one would know where they were from or what they left behind.

*   *   *

After traveling by foot for a week, they found a small village in Chiapas where they lived and grew their family. Santiago had been educated by the church and shared his knowledge with his new wife. Together they prospered in the village where no one knew who they were, only that they were kind folk who wanted to live their lives in peace. Ikal, the father of Ix Chel. Ix Chel and Santiago, the ancestors of Milagros.

CHAPTER SIXTEEN

The Queen had visited my son and placed a story in his mind. Like everything from her, it was not fiction. There was no doubt in my mind it was the past. I had not feared her until now. I dug into my bag to find a compact with a mirror.

"La Reina de Las Chicharras chicharrachicharrachicharra."

I waited for her to show her face in the mirror. Nothing. I closed the compact. In my periphery vision, there she stood. Her flayed body was adorned with jade, gold, feathers and turquoise.

"Hello and congratulations on the birth of your daughters. You have done so well. I want to reward you."

If I wasn't in so much pain from my stitches, I would have stood to face her.

"Tell me your plans. If you want to claim another soul, take mine."

She cocked her head and frowned. "I have not harmed any of your children. It is not my intention now or ever. Jacob is an apostle of sorts; you must have read the tale he wrote. Isn't it beautiful? It tells you the roots of Milagros and her special ancestral blood. In time your son will be a priest like Hector. Jacob is still young and has much life to live. Hector's bloodline, my bloodline and the blood of Ikal are immensely powerful. Not in a hundred universes did I think this was possible. Three outstanding strands of DNA. And your daughter with Arie will recover. People have great regard for her father but she will eclipse him in many ways. Milagros Ix Chel has her own special path."

For a moment I doubted myself. Maybe I was wrong not to fear this goddess taking over the world by captivating people's hearts and imaginations. "What are you doing? What is any of this? It makes no sense to me. I have given of myself freely."

I think she sensed my desperation and anger. She stepped closer, leaving bloody footprints in her wake. An ankle bracelet of tiny bird bones and shells clinked with her every move, which were as smooth as trickling water.

"I'm rebuilding my church and this broken, wayward world. You see, I was sacrificed as an infant in the universe that I call home. Milagros was sacrificed without her consent. You might choose to make a sacrifice and your offspring will be blessed from all of this. Milagros Ix Chel and her siblings will save humankind before the ash of your bones is all that covers this world. There won't even be bones for me to claim or enough for the god you call Jesus to blow life into. Don't you want your bloodline to herald in a new cycle for humankind? Because this world needs to see that we must all sacrifice for each other to survive." The Queen was now at my bedside, both pairs of our breasts leaking colostrum.

"I am death and I see death. As you know, I have shown potential worshippers their own final breath so they may prove their devotion to me and live in a way that will make a difference for themselves or those around them." She leaned in, pressing her lips against mine. It was what I wanted since kissing her in the bathroom. Her mouth nearly took my breath away as she opened her jaw wide enough to swallow me whole, yet it was just her tongue that danced with mine. I swear I could see the stars, the place where she was from. And then my next purpose was revealed the deeper we kissed. My son wrote 'The Book of Ikal', Hector would write 'The Life of Milagros Ix Chel' and I would write 'The Book of Mictecacíhuatl: Queen of Bones'. My words were not meaningless fragments.

All this had to be done before it was too late. But I knew I couldn't accomplish this work on Earth, in this form and held back by my skin. Her story needed me elsewhere. I needed to see in a way that humans were not allowed to see.

Then she gave me a parting vision that broke my soul. I had a decision to make. Do I leave this place to give my children and future generations life? Watching their death was like a small death inside of me that I won't ever forget, but it was also a gift. Many times, I had felt I had failed Jacob, and I would not fail him now. I had the power to change the course of horrible events that he would experience with his sister. Jacob would soon be a man. My daughter had her father. Not once did Arie and I say we loved each other. In some ways we did, but we loved each other's bodies more, for the time it lasted. How long before that faded as all things do? He was a good man. I knew he would care for and cherish our daughter, whom I had not even named.

The Queen pulled her mouth away from mine, allowing me to taste my tears. "Now you can forever be with your children and they, along with Hector and Milagros Ix Chel, will be in our care. Always protected."

With tears still flowing from my eyes, I shook my head. I hadn't had the opportunity yet to touch my daughter with Arie, who was in an incubator. Making this sacrifice would mean I never would. However, my fate was in the stars all along, and it was that place I would return to. I had to accept that Jacob and I would never go on that vacation; I couldn't hold him one last time; I would never be flesh at any of the big events of any of my children's lives. These experiences could only be mine in spirit. But I was still their mother and would always be their mother. The decision was made.

"I'm ready, but I need to say goodbye."

I wrote letters with double breast pumps attached to my breasts to leave little Milagros Ix Chel and my daughter a parting gift. Hector and my son would need some explanation for my sudden departure, as would Arie for our child. I assured them I would always be near even if they could only hear and see me occasionally. Hector and Arie would understand because they were believers. This world was spinning out of control in a universe that would continue to expand without it in it, without *us* in it. Everything moved in cycles and our Queen was here to help usher in a new cycle before the final destruction occurred. There was a reason Arie and I met and created our daughter. The stars. When I finished pumping and writing, I called the Queen from my compact mirror.

Mictecacíhuatl appeared at my bedside. She moved close enough again to kiss me hard. A searing pain erupted from within my chest. I looked down to see my beating heart in her hand and a hole through my ribcage, yet I was still alive.

"Come with me," she whispered.

I placed my hand over hers as my heart continued to beat. We squeezed it together, the blood running down our forearms. It began to shrink and harden until it was a smooth stone of jade in my hand. This would go to my son.

"We can go now." I left the stone next to the note for Jacob. My body slumped in the hospital bed, breasts still leaking milk from my bloody, open chest. My time as a vessel was over and it was time for me to become a storyteller.

Without skin I will fly.

EPILOGUE

"Don't! Don't! Please, I'm pregnant! My daughter is here! We have papers! Please! I only work at the chicken factory part-time," shouted Mommy.

"We're investigating everyone. If everything turns out fine you and your children will be reunited. For now, you're coming with us."

Manuela's body shook with terror. She thought she might wet herself, and she hadn't done that since she was a baby. She was a big girl now, a smart and brave girl as her mother liked to say. But today as she got ready for school these strange men in black knocked on the door loudly and now tried to take her away from her mommy. Her father was at work making his deliveries. How would he know where to find them? They already took Mommy's phone away, so she couldn't call anyone for help, including their lawyer. Whatever a lawyer was.

Mommy stood defiantly in front of her, legs spread wide like a pyramid, chest moving up and down from heavy breathing. The flap where her shirt was torn from the struggle waved at Manuela. The men tried to tear them apart, but Mommy wouldn't let them. Another man with black rubber gloves that made his hands look like something from a monster film entered the house through the open front door.

"Come on. We don't want to press charges. We can make your situation worse."

"Worse? What is worse than strangers ripping a family apart! ¡Pinche tu madre!"

Manuela could see their faces turn to stone or empty Halloween masks. They would be rough now. In her hand she clutched a doll that held a pink plastic mirror. It was a sticker, but she could still see the reflection of one eye. Manuela didn't want to be taken away, not now or ever. This was the only home she knew. She remembered a story her auntie told her mother during one of their family barbeques.

Both men pulled at her mother's arms.

Mommy screamed like a wildcat or a bear on one of those nature shows she liked to watch. "No, no, no!"

Manuela was beginning to panic, her body still shaking. She was going to cry and wet herself. She yelled with every breath left in her eight-year-old little lungs while looking in the doll's mirror, "La Reina de Las Chicharras! Chicharrachicharrachicharra! Help us! Kill these bad men!"

The men ignored her, still pulling on her mother, leaving red marks on her arms. Then the lights flickered above their heads, the front door slammed in the face of the social worker about to walk in. The locks clicked.

"The fuck?" One of the ICE officers let her mother go. The other followed his lead.

"When my name is called, I must show myself."

A woman emerged from the kitchen in dirty clothes not from this time, a red bandanna around her mouth. Parts of her skull and skin were missing.

"Miss, are you all right?" one of the officers asked. "We're here with ICE. You'll come with us now. How many more are in the house?"

The voice of another woman that was neither human nor animal spoke to them. "Just me."

Mommy crossed herself and pushed her body against Manuela

again. Manuela could still see. This other woman had no skin, but she wasn't scary; she was beautiful, with green feathers in her hair and necklaces around her neck. She looked directly at Manuela, giving her a smile and a nod with her hand over her exposed beating heart. Manuela wanted to run to her and touch it. Just like in science class.

"I've crossed borders to be here. Would you like to take me in, officers?"

The two men stumbled in the dark with their faces twisted in dread.

"Get away! What are you?"

"Holy shit! Holy shit, it's true! God help us!" screamed one of the officers.

Both women laughed. "Your god hears and sees and your god is not pleased, hence the silence. You are now left with me."

The woman in the bandana and the skinless one ignored the mother and child as they cornered the officers. Before one could reach for his firearm, the woman in jeans pulled down her bandana, releasing insects into the air. Mommy crouched, making a shield with her body, but Manuela could still see. Out of the stinging horde that attacked the wailing, thrashing men, a butterfly and chicharra flew away to rest on her mother's knee.

"Look, Mama," Manuela whispered. "They aren't scared, so we shouldn't be scared. They will protect us."

Her mother looked at her through puffy wet eyes, then at the butterfly and the chicharra. The creatures playfully fluttered together. "I will always protect you and your sister inside of me. I think we should call her Mariposa, to remember this day."

The ICE officers pulled and beat on the front door until suddenly it opened on its own, releasing the insects. Manuela could hear a woman scream outside, then screeching wheels. Good. They were safe again.

The woman in the bandana and jeans looked back at Manuela.

Without moving her lips, she spoke to her inside her head. "I will see you soon. I will be one of you again."

Manuela felt warm inside of her tummy and heart. She thought it might be what adults called hope.

FLAME TREE PRESS
FICTION WITHOUT FRONTIERS
Award-Winning Authors & Original Voices

Flame Tree Press is the trade fiction imprint of Flame Tree Publishing, focusing on excellent writing in horror and the supernatural, crime and mystery, science fiction and fantasy. Our aim is to explore beyond the boundaries of the everyday, with tales from both award-winning authors and original voices.

•

•

Join our mailing list for free short stories, new release details, news about our authors and special promotions:

flametreepress.com